DATE DUE

FEB 1 2 2007			
MAY 2 4 2010			
GAYLORD			PRINTED IN U.S.A.

Emily Goldberg Learns to SALSA

Emily Goldberg Learns to SALSA

Micol Ostow

razor
bill

Emily Goldberg Learns to Salsa

RAZORBILL

Published by the Penguin Group
Penguin Young Readers Group
345 Hudson Street, New York, New York 10014, U.S.A.
Penguin Group (USA) Inc., 375 Hudson Street, New York, New York 10014, U.S.A.
Penguin Group (Canada), 90 Eglinton Avenue East, Suite 700, Toronto, Ontario, Canada M4P 2Y3
(a division of Pearson Penguin Canada Inc.)
Penguin Books Ltd, 80 Strand, London WC2R 0RL, England
Penguin Ireland, 25 St Stephen's Green, Dublin 2, Ireland (a division of Penguin Books Ltd)
Penguin Group (Australia), 250 Camberwell Road, Camberwell, Victoria 3124, Australia
(a division of Pearson Australia Group Pty Ltd)
Penguin Books India Pvt Ltd, 11 Community Centre, Panchsheel Park, New Delhi – 110 017, India
Penguin Group (NZ), Cnr Airborne and Rosedale Roads, Albany, Auckland 1310, New Zealand
(a division of Pearson New Zealand Ltd)
Penguin Books (South Africa) (Pty) Ltd, 24 Sturdee Avenue, Rosebank,
Johannesburg 2196, South Africa

Penguin Books Ltd, Registered Offices: 80 Strand, London WC2R 0RL, England

10 9 8 7 6 5 4 3 2 1

Library of Congress Cataloging-in-Publication Data is available

Printed in the United States of America

To my mother, the original boriqua *babe.*

One

It's hot.

It's very hot.

Inexplicably, it is about three thousand degrees in this overstuffed funeral home, a fact that is not abetted by the number of sweat-shiny mourners pressed against one another, fanning themselves.

At the front of the room is my grandmother Rosa's casket, propped open in full display. I did not know my grandmother Rosa, and I did not, until this very day, have any idea that my mother's extended family was so large.

There are probably a hundred or so relatives at this wake and at least fifty too many stuffed into this room. A rickety fan whirs forlornly in the far corner, but it's too far away to do much good from where I sit. I don't think it's doing anything other than stirring the thick, heavy air anyway. Everyone is clamoring to get closer to the casket, to finger the rosary beads interlaced through my grandmother's unfeeling fingers, to glance from the framed photo that stands on a small side table to my grandmother and back to the photo again.

I hear murmurs, reviews of her lifelike appearance. But I never knew my grandmother in life, so I am not in a position to comment.

This is a day of firsts, my grandmother's body being only one of the several things I am seeing for the very first time today: Puerto Rico, a wake, an open casket, rosary beads. My mother's family, the Ramírezes.

My father, brother, Max, and I stand at the very back of the room and try not to look self-conscious. This is no easy feat. We could not stand out more if we were wearing matching neon jumpsuits.

There is a trick I picked up back, I think, on the first day of middle school, a trick to looking like you aren't feeling out of place. The trick is to stand very, very still and be very, very quiet.

Sometimes people see this behavior and assume—mistakenly—that you are supremely pissed off. But it's all about getting the lay of the land. Looking at my mother, who stands just next to the casket, holding one of her three sisters' hands, I think that it will take more time than I can even imagine to get the lay of *this* land.

Sometimes people take me for being aloof or even stuck-up, I know. At least they did in school before they got to know me, before they realized that I was just shy. But being stuck-up is infinitely better than sticking out, I think.

My mother runs her fingertips along the smooth, polished wood of the casket. She looks confused. Behind her stand her three older sisters, all jostling to get closer to the body. They remind me of a set of dolls I had as a child, identical wooden carvings that grew successively smaller, each cradled inside the doll one larger until, ultimately, they were all swallowed by the largest. A matched set.

My mother and her sisters have the same cocoa-colored skin, the same rich brown eyes, the same thick dark hair.

It is like watching the results of some elaborate long-term psychological study, the ones with the twins separated at birth. After being raised under vastly polarized circumstances, they come back together to discover that they are inherently the same nonetheless.

I know the story: my mother came to New York as a coed, the only one of her sisters to go to college. What I don't know is whether or not she ever planned to return to Puerto Rico. She met my father during her sophomore year and married him just after they graduated. She got her PhD in women's studies and a cushy position at a CUNY outpost; he went to law school. At some point they fled the city in pursuit of the suburban yuppie dream: an SUV, a Sub-Zero refrigerator, private school for myself and for Max. I shouldn't sound so bitchy, though; I never minded it. The only thing I didn't have was contact with my mother's family.

Over the years I'd formed my own opinions as to why that was. In my mind the situation morphs into a glamorous if tragic melodrama, a Cinderella story of a self-made woman forced to choose between two lives. Surveying the sea of ill-fitting suits, scuffed shoes, and wrinkled faces before me, I think I can understand why she made the choice that she did. If only she didn't look so miserable.

To my right, Max elbows me in the ribs. "I think someone's getting set to speak."

I follow his gaze. Indeed, at the front of the room, a stocky man, bursting out of his best outfit, is pushing off from his seat. My brother raises his eyebrows to show what he thinks of this development. "Let's go while the going's good." He turns to my father and tugs at his suit jacket. "We have to hit the bathroom."

My dad pivots and shoots us both a pleading look. He stands stiffly, at least three paces from the nearest relative. He clearly does not want to be left alone. But really, we're all three of us alone here together. There isn't much I can do for him in this room at this moment as this surreal scene unfolds.

Also, I think I'm melting deep into the waistband of my matte jersey skirt. Gross.

"We'll be right back," I whisper to my dad, not necessarily meaning it. I pat his back reassuringly, and Max and I slip out the back exit, unnoticed.

"Your grandmother passed away last night," my father said to me. "It was a heart attack, in the middle of the night."

I panicked, my breath coming in short bursts, reminding me suddenly of young women in Victorian times, laced tight into cage-like corsets.

How could this be? I thought. Nana wasn't old, not by grandparents standards. We'd had dinner together last Friday night, the same as we do every week. She bought a challah from the local kosher bakery, and her housekeeper roasted a chicken. We waited for dinner to be ready while my grandfather listened to classical music in his library.

Max and I sat in the living room, pretending not to be arguing over whether we'd watch reruns of The Simpsons *or* Friends. *Business as usual. No sign of trouble, heart or otherwise.*

But there it was, Tuesday, a random Tuesday afternoon.

I sat at the kitchen table scratching a pencil over the surface of a crossword puzzle. It was a thoroughly unremarkable day but for the fact that my grandmother was now dead. Max and my mother were nowhere to be found. Maybe they'd already heard?

"When is the funeral?" I asked. I swallowed hard.

"Saturday," he replied. "We'll leave for Puerto Rico tomorrow morning." Then, as an afterthought, "You should pack."

There were a million bits and pieces of that sentence that were wrong. I couldn't even pinpoint them, couldn't decide where to begin. For one, there was the fact that according to Jewish tradition, a funeral must be held as soon after a death as possible. Saturday wasn't soon: it was three days away.

Also unclear to me was why we would be packing for Puerto Rico. This was—to say the least—not an ideal time to be taking a vacation. I struggled with these thoughts, deliberating how best to voice these concerns. I rearranged my features as best as I could, aiming for some sort of neutral countenance. To fall apart right then would have been some sort of watershed, and I wasn't ready for that.

After a few false starts, I settled on, "Huh?"

It was my father's turn to be baffled. He was drinking from a glass of water and played a thick finger along the rim of the glass, slowly scrunching up his forehead. For a few minutes he didn't say anything. I guessed that like me, he was trying very hard to hold it together. Suddenly, though, the creases in his face settled themselves, deflating into a smooth, uninterrupted landscape. I recognized that look. It was dawning realization.

"Oh," he said, taking a slow sip from his glass and gulping it down with great effort. "No."

"No, what?"

Now I was impatient. No, she's not dead? No, there's no funeral? No, we will not be having an awkwardly timed trip? Was this all a huge mistake?

"No, sweetie. You're misunderstanding. Not that grandma. It's Grandma Rosa that's dead."

Outside of the funeral parlor, Max points out a thicket of shrubbery in desperate need of watering. "Here," he says, and ducks behind it. He digs into his pocket and pulls out a pack of Marlboros. He fishes a cigarette from the pack and a lighter from his other pocket. In one deft motion, the cigarette is lit. All at once he's inhaling in quick, thick gulps. He turns his face from me and exhales forcefully, a steady stream of smoke, more of a sigh than anything else. He runs his free hand through his hair. "Jesus."

I nod. Mostly I'm stunned that he's got the whole routine down to under ten seconds—my brother, the high school freshman.

I wonder what else he knows how to do. At the same time, I don't want to ask.

I realize I'm feeling slightly dizzy from the heat. The

fresh air is a relief, but the sun beats down mercilessly. The humidity is cloying. The atmosphere hangs on me like wet cotton. I am very resentful of the fact that I am wearing stockings; I'm, like, the only one here who is. Other than my mother, of course.

Max gestures toward a collection of children playing a makeshift game—it looks like it could be jacks or maybe marbles—over near a spindly bush of their own. The girls' braids are coming undone, and the boys' shoes are untied. The toys that they are playing with strike the ground and cough up clouds of dust, causing everyone to laugh.

"Who *are* these people?" he continues, taking another drag.

"Our family," I say. Which makes me laugh, for some reason.

He shrugs. "It's weird."

I agree, but *weird* does not even begin to cover it. "Sunday feels very far away."

Sunday is when we leave. Between now and then, who knows? Other than the funeral, which is tomorrow, I have no idea what we're going to do. Besides, I have an entire life waiting for me back in Westchester. Friends. Plans. Boys. Or rather, one boy.

Now it's Max's turn to nod. "Did you talk to Noah?"

"Of course," I say, choosing not to get into it. Noah is

the boy in question. My boyfriend. I would not have skipped the country—the continental United States, that is—without letting him know. But I'd rather not replay our conversation just now.

"I thought you didn't have much contact with them," he'd said.

It was the understatement of the century. We've been in Puerto Rico for a cool twelve hours and the most contact I've had with anyone other than my father, my mother, or Max was five minutes ago, when I brushed past a blond girl who looked vaguely my age as Max and I hightailed it out of the funeral home.

I look out to the street in front of the funeral home. This is not the Puerto Rico of getaway brochures. The blacktop is patchy and crumbling in places, as though there were plans to repave that haven't been seen through. Scraggly weeds dot the road on either side. Across the street is a strip mall. I count one pizza place, two taquerias, and a 7-Eleven. A stop sign on the corner has been sprayed with graffiti. The first taqueria, the one with the bolder, brighter sign, is boarded up. They will not be opening this afternoon.

"Can I bum one of those?"

I turn my head to find the blond girl from inside. She is looking at my brother questioningly. He fumbles for a moment, awkward, then reaches into his pocket for her. She lights her own cigarette and sucks at it greedily.

Now she looks at me.

"You don't smoke?" she asks.

I shake my head. "Never have." This is not exactly true. I tried it once at a party, erupted into a hugely embarrassing choking fit, and have not touched cigarettes since. But the finer points of my experiments with controlled substances are no one's business but my own, right?

She levels me with a steady gaze. "Good girl," she says, taking a slow drag. She makes this sound like she's talking about more than just smoking. Like she's maybe insulting me. I shoot her my best non-expression.

"You're Gloria's kids," she says. This is not a question.

"Uh-huh," Max says. He's cool as a cucumber, too cool for school, way too cool for his older sister, who is starting to feel like something out of the *Twilight Zone*. Is this jet lag, a time difference thing? I check my watch: no dice. We're on regular old EST.

"I'm Lucy. Domingo. You know, Rosa's daughter," she says. She extends a hand, presumably for us to shake, and we do, in slow, slightly suspicious succession. She jerks her head toward the funeral home. "What do you think of the wake?" she asks.

"It's a party," Max says lightly. I know he feels as out of

place as I do, but still—he's not at all intimidated by Lucy, not at all intimidated by this landscape. I am wildly, fitfully jealous. I haven't said three words since we stepped off the plane. I keep arranging and rearranging words in my head, but they sound ten different kinds of wrong, so I bite them back.

Even when Rosa, Lucy's mother, I now learn, approached me inside, I choked. She hugged me like we weren't two strangers who had met only moments before. She threw her arms around me like we were family. What could I say to that?

"It's the first you've been to, right?" she continues.

"Uh-huh." I shrug. "The first wake."

"Is it different than a Jewish funeral?"

She over-enunciates the word *Jewish*. It comes out like two totally separate words tacked together with some sort of verbal Scotch tape. I imagine myself imitating that pronunciation to Isabelle and Adrienne when I get back, then squash the plan on the grounds of it being evil and gossipy.

Max casually tosses his cigarette to the pavement and stomps it out with his heel. "Well, yeah. We don't do the open casket," he said. "This is like something you see on TV."

A flash of anger flickers across her face. I'm immediately defensive—*You asked, didn't you?* But then I think back to how I reacted when my father first told me my grandmother was dead, how upset I was, before I realized just who, exactly, he meant.

"We haven't, um, been to any wakes," I jump in, hoping to diffuse the situation.

"Right," Max says, waving his hand in front of his face impatiently. "Is this what they're all like?"

Now Lucy looks fully irritated. "I don't know. This is the first one I've been to," she snaps.

The door to the building swings open and a compact woman with hair the color of orange juice peeks her head out. "Lucy! We need you in here! Someone has to help put out the empanadas!"

Lucy drops her cigarette in an instant, grinds her heel onto it surreptitiously.

Very smooth, I think. I could learn something from a girl like this.

Maybe I could stand to learn something.

"Coming!" she calls back, sweet and bright. To us she says, "Nice to meet you."

It's impossible to tell from her expression whether or not she means this, but I can guess. Before we can reply, she turns and rushes back into the funeral home.

I glare at Max.

"What?" he asks innocently.

"You pissed her off. That was insensitive."

He holds his hands out, palms up, the picture of innocence. "Do you care?"

I open my mouth to reply but close it again swiftly. It's an interesting question. I don't know. And I'm not going back inside until I have to.

I'm in no mood to watch my father fidget nervously, and I'm not prepared to see my mother cry. Again. I'm not used to it and I can't handle it. And clearly Max and I have nothing to offer our long-lost relatives by way of comfort or understanding.

The sight of the casket, too, is disturbing. In part because it's the only time I've ever been up close and personal with a dead body, sure, but in part because there's a nagging feeling inside me, a sense of loss. And that confuses me entirely. How can you lose something you never had to begin with?

When Rosa hugged me, I felt awkward, of course. How could you not, smothered by a near stranger? But there were other emotions lingering beneath the surface too. Emotions that startled me. Her warmth was . . . comforting. But why did I need comfort for someone I'd never known? Lucy needed comfort way more than I did. She was the one whose *abuelita* had died. Which may have explained why her distrust and attitude felt warranted somehow.

I glance at the children in the corner. They have abandoned their toys and are now busy constructing some sort of sculpture over in the dirt heap. They're speaking rapid-fire Spanish that I can't make out from where I'm standing.

Three years of honors language classes and I'm useless at a distance of more than five feet. I briefly contemplate joining them over on the ground—I was a whiz at sand castles when I was younger—but remember I'm still wearing stockings. And even if I weren't, it's way too hot for that this afternoon.

So instead I gaze at them, continuing to appear utterly unconcerned.

Two

aturday morning. I awake to a room that's thick with darkness. But I'm bright-eyed, and so it must be morning. My body clock is never wrong. I sit up, adjusting, and then it hits me.

Puerto Rico. I'm in Puerto Rico. We're staying on Isla Verde, which I know is a top resort beach. Isabelle and Adrienne were optimistic when they heard, helped me choose a super-skimpy bikini for the suitcase, something I can't believe I own and would certainly never wear. On the bed next to mine Max snores heavily. I'm surprised the noise didn't wake me sooner. I guess I was more tired than I realized.

I tiptoe out of bed and toward the window, peeking my head tentatively underneath the blackout curtain. I'm rewarded with a burst of sunlight so strong that I physically recoil. The ocean glitters. I glance toward the clock on my nightstand: 8:05. I'm not sure what the day's itinerary is, but I'm pretty sure nothing major is going to go down for at least another hour or two. And I am in Puerto Rico, after all.

What was it that Max said at the wake? "It's a party"?

I quietly make my way toward my suitcase, groping inside it in the dark. In a moment I've fished out a swimsuit—not the one that Ade and Izzy picked out, but something sportier, sturdier.

I could use something sturdy, I think. Today I'm feeling a bit insubstantial.

"You're going where?" Adrienne asked, her brows knit together in confusion. "When?"

"Puerto Rico," I said for the second time, working a nail file across the jagged edge of the thumbnail I'd been chewing all afternoon. "Tomorrow."

"It's your grandma that died?" Isabelle asked.

"Yes." I put the nail file down and looked at them both. Adrienne was flopped backward in the oversized rocking chair my mother rescued from a neighborhood yard sale; Isabelle was sprawled on her stomach, flipping idly through a magazine. Both seemed only mildly concerned about this development. But it was hard to expect them to get particu-

larly upset about someone I had never really even mentioned before.

"I told you my mother's family was Puerto Rican," I said, stating the obvious.

"Yeah, but . . ." Adrienne trailed off. "You never talk about them."

"I never have anything to say."

Understatement. Huge, honking understatement.

Isabelle drummed her fingers against her magazine. "You'll be back next week?"

I nodded. "We're just going for the funeral. It's Saturday. And I guess we'll stay the weekend. But Dad promises I'll be back in time to catch whatever cheesy blockbuster is opening next weekend." I felt slightly guilty that the trip seemed little more than an inconvenience. But then, it wasn't my fault that I'd never met my mother's family.

"Good," Isabelle said. "Because we need to start packing for our trip."

The vacation had been Izzy's idea, a six-week, cross-country spree. "Like Thelma and Louise. Except without the crime and the death," she said.

"Or Brad Pitt," Ade pointed out helpfully.

"You never know." Isabelle wagged her eyebrows suggestively. She'd broken up with Ryan, her boyfriend, ages ago, just after Christmas break. We'd all been shocked since they were Woodland's alpha couple. But Izzy was nothing if not pragmatic: "Please. Like we're going to stay together when we're off at separate colleges? Better to get this over with now so we can enjoy our senior year, right?"

"Right," Ade had affirmed.

Unlike myself, Adrienne hated to be tethered to one guy. She didn't sleep around, but she definitely liked male attention. Isabelle didn't mind—as long as she and her relationships were still the main focus of Adrienne's attention.

Personally, I preferred to be out of the spotlight. Noah and I had started dating in September, and it was my first real relationship. He was totally hot—I had noticed him the year before, when he transferred in from a prep school in Connecticut—and while I wasn't surprised that he asked me out, in some ways he was different than I expected my first boyfriend to be.

Noah was louder, with a confident laugh and a pronounced stride. But he was thoughtful when we were alone together. Like it was some huge secret that he wasn't a total Y-chromosomed jerk. He played soccer with Ryan and some other guys we hung with, which put him in some sort of comfort zone or something, so Izzy and Ade were totally supportive.

I had worried briefly when Isabelle broke up with Ryan that it'd be awkward, me having a boyfriend, but the stressing turned out to be totally pointless. Izzy was cool with being sin-gle, and Ade was always being pursued by a million different guys. For the most part, our Saturday nights didn't change one bit: that is, we still spent them at the mall or the movie theater or camped out in the basement of whoever's parents' house for the night or, if we were lucky, the weekend. The boys—including Ryan and Noah—were just there with us. And I enjoyed it—a lot—even if somewhere, somehow, I wondered if there wasn't a deeper level of connection that Noah and I were missing.

Sometime around March, Izzy had hit on the idea of a road trip. Just the three of us, over the summer. A sort of gradu-ation present to ourselves. We'd go cross-country in her SUV, which wasn't so environmentally conscious but was still the best shot we had at actually making it to sunny Cal. Adrienne shared her car with her younger sister, who would definitely not be okay with saying good-bye to her wheels all summer long. My own vehicle, a cute two-door, was not only too small for our purposes but too "previously owned" as well. Not Thelma and Louise *material.*

When I first told my parents about the trip, they balked. *Yadda yadda job, yadda yadda preparing for college, yadda yadda soon you'll be off at Brown and we'll never see you.* Then my father made the grave tactical error of invoking "the dan-gers of three women alone on the road together." The look on

Mom's face told me I could start packing any old time.

A week after that conversation she took me to the local mechanic's and taught me how to change a tire. And upgraded my Triple-A service.

Noah said he'd miss me but agreed that the trip sounded awesome. Being separated for six weeks over the summer made me slightly nervous. We had studiously avoided any discussion of "us, post-high school," and I wasn't totally sure where, if anywhere, "we" were going—but the trip was definitely an opportunity not to be missed. Newly inaugurated into the cult of roadside assistance, I bought a slew of maps and budget-conscious guidebooks with cute, quirky titles. We plotted our entire trip—three weeks one way, three weeks back, barring unforeseen catastrophe.

We were set to leave a week from Friday. A week from my grandmother's funeral. Grandma Rosa, that was.

"I know, I need to pack, but like I said, the funeral is tomorrow. We are coming back on Sunday. That gives me four whole days when I get back. It's no problem." What would I need other than a few pair of cutoffs and some tank tops?

Isabelle looked doubtful. I knew it would take her at least a week just to pare down the contents of her closet.

"Like Sophie's Choice. *But with clothes," as she would put it.*

"Isabelle. Come on. Emily's right."

Adrienne, our own personal reality check.

"It's Thursday. And it's just going to be us three on the road."

"But you have to be prepared for any contingency," Iz insisted.

"Right. Disco gear, scuba gear, spelunking gear, drag-race gear," I teased. *"On the list. Every possible contingency. In fact, you two should get started—that way I can just follow your lead."*

"You're so funny," she said, deadpan.

"Monday," I promised. *"Monday I will break out my all-purpose wear."*

* * *

Surprisingly, I am not the only person out on the beach this early. I pass a scattering of sunbathers stretched across lounge chairs, working on their tans as though it were a paying job: shoulders squared and greased. Max and I usually brown, even without meaning to; one long bike ride and our cheeks are flushed bronze. Until now, that's as close as we've come to our inner Ramírezes.

I don't blame my mom, necessarily, for cutting us off from her former life. Which is not the same as saying that I understand why she made the choice she did. But I respect it, I guess. I don't imagine that her family had very much money. I don't think her sisters went to college. I don't know if they encouraged her to pursue a career. So maybe she thought a separation was the only way out? The only way to get ahead?

I'm only guessing here. Reaching. These are assumptions. Point being, my mom's decision was just that—her own.

I don't resent her choice. But it puts me in a curious position right now, feeling like an interloper among my own family. Affected by a death but not feeling entitled to my emotions.

I step past the early birds and make my way to the water's edge, dipping my toe in tentatively. It's warm enough to bathe in. I make my way slowly down the shoreline, taking in the expanse of hotels, bars, and restaurants. It's clear we are in serious tourist territory here, but two blocks out it's strip-mall city. My mother says the locals still like Isla Verde, even though it's not totally their own anymore.

She told us this at the airport, just as we boarded the plane. As if she'd been here recently—as if she knew.

There is a breeze playing off the surface of the ocean that brushes my hair off my face. The air feels light here by the water, not humid and cloying like it is on the beaches in New York. It's deceptive, I know. The breeze brings the temperature down by five degrees or so. It makes you forget how hot the sun is down here, so close to the equator. It's a false sense of security, the atmosphere along the shoreline. In weather like this, you could easily forget about sunscreen. But then you'd burn in an instant. Before you even realized what was happening.

* * *

Dinner is at our aunt Rosa's, my mother's next-oldest sister. It goes Amalia, Eva, Rosa, Gloria. My mother, Gloria, is the youngest. I just learned this the other day, after the wake, after seeing my mother and her sisters all lined up in a row. Watching them together, it is nearly impossible to discern the birth order. My mother's face is smoothest, but beyond that it's anyone's guess. Eva has two sons, Carlos and Juan, both of whom are gargantuan, muscled, and near silent. Rosa's son, José, waved to me grudgingly at the funeral but only when prompted by his mother, who waved at *my* mother only slightly less grudgingly. And unlike the myriad of female cousins that I've just discovered, these boys are nowhere to be found at dinner.

When we arrive, it's chaos, a mass of bodies weaving in and out of each other, some carrying plastic cups and paper plates, some balancing wriggling babies on ample hips. The women are at work multitasking—barking into the telephone, wiping grimy young faces, tossing trash into large plastic bags. Lucy is among them, I note without surprise, wiping down countertops efficiently. The men—vastly out-numbered—are for the most part gathered around an ancient television tuned to a Spanish variety show. On-screen, redheads in halter tops chirp brightly and gesticulate with lacquered fingernails.

Max just shakes his head. I'm sure he's dying for a smoke, but there's nowhere for him to disappear to. He knows my mother would freak out—and now is really not the time to test her.

"How long do you think we're staying?" he asks. He has a copy of *Ulysses* in his jacket pocket, but he wouldn't dare break it out in plain sight. Ten bucks says he cracks before the end of the night—crouches in a bathroom or under a table to knock off a chapter or two. Funny that he hides his reading as furtively as he does his smoking.

Or maybe that's sort of sad, considering. Other kids do drugs; my brother hides his classics habit.

"Are you hungry?" my dad asks. "There's a ton of food." He shrugs his shoulder in the general direction of the kitchen.

I tiptoe toward the madhouse of meal preparation. A wave of thick, dense air ripe with cooking smells hits me dead on. Every square inch of the room is covered with peo-ple, not one of whom I recognize.

Wham.

I recoil as my big toe is smashed into the floor. An involuntary "ow" escapes me.

"Perdón, lo siento—" My assaulter stops short. Her brown eyes flash.

"Lucy," I realize.

"Emily." She does not look pleased to see me. "Excuse me." She steps around me awkwardly, raising her arms so as not to hit me with the platter of fried bananas that she is carrying.

"Emily."

Another platter—much heavier than it looks—is placed in my arms. Lucy's mother, Rosa, levels me with a gaze. *"Diga a los muchachos que necesitan comer ahora."*

She could be speaking Martian for all I understand. The edges of the platter dig into the flesh of my inner forearms.

"¿Sí? ¿Y qué es el problema?"

This time I know exactly what she's saying. But I'm choking somehow on my tongue, tripping on the words. I can't think of what to say or how. What *is* my problem?

"Emily."

I look up. This time it's my mother. I'm expecting her to be at least semi-amused by my ineptitude, but instead her face is blank, her eyes hollow and tired. "Emily, take the *plátanos* to the living room. Where Lucy went."

To Rosa she says, "She doesn't speak Spanish."

Mute, I backtrack carefully out into the melee, leading hip first over to the chipped Formica table where Lucy has laid her platter. I set mine down beside it. Lucy has her back to me, but she turns when she hears me.

"Thanks," she says automatically. "My mom asked you to?" It's an observation, not a question. I nod. Like there's no other way I'd be pitching in. I guess I'm not as . . . *domestic* as she is.

Max shuffles over to investigate. "Bananas?" He leans into the steaming towers of grease-slicked fruit and sniffs.

"*Plátanos,*" Lucy corrects him.

He spears one with a plastic fork, shoves it into his mouth, chews thoughtfully for a moment or two. "Bananas," he decides after he's swallowed. "Not very ripe." He puts down his fork and wanders off.

Lucy stares after him for a beat, then back down to the table. Pointedly she picks up his fork and drops it in the nearest garbage can.

I shrug. "He's fourteen," I say, as though he couldn't possibly know better.

"*You're* not," she counters.

And she's gone.

It occurs to me that Lucy doesn't much like me. It's an uncommon situation for me to be in. Avoiding conflict is sort of my thing. I'd rather gnaw my own arm off at the elbow than challenge Lucy on her words or call Noah out for being late to pick me up on a Saturday night.

Pathetic but true. What can I say? I hate tension. And the tension here is thick as Elmer's glue.

I survey the scene once more: Max has abandoned me, no doubt curled up clandestinely with James Joyce. My father is settled precariously on the edge of an overstuffed couch, concentrating aggressively on the variety show. The big-haired women have been replaced by a dog on a unicycle accompanied by a mariachi player. My only recourse, I decide, is a bathroom break.

When I emerge from the powder room, I find my mother huddled against the wall with Rosa and Eva. Eva's eyes are red-rimmed, and she's sniffling. My mother supports her with one arm around Eva's waist. Rosa pats Eva's shoulder. Rosa and my mother seem uncomfortable with each other. Then again, *uncomfortable* seems to be the norm here.

"*Mira,* it's the *nuyorican!*" Rosa laughs. It's clearly an attempt to cheer Eva up. She reaches out, and for one horrifying moment I actually think she's going to pinch my ass, but instead she merely grabs my cheek—the one on my face—between her thumb and forefinger and squeezes. It's all I can do not to cry out. My abject terror must be obvious because she cackles even more wildly, her whole body shaking with the exertion. *"Te enseñare-mos el español, mamita,"* she says. "We'll teach you Spanish yet."

"She took it in school," my mother says, expressionless.

"I did," I say lamely. "I got an A."

We leave before I'm desperate enough to try a fried plantain or a piece of chorizo. We wrest Max from the tiny basement bedroom he has discovered—Joyce has been highlighted many passages over—and cab it back to the hotel. My father wants a good night's sleep so he can be fresh for travel tomorrow morning. Our flight is at 1 p.m., but he'll be up by eight, packing.

Later, much later, as I lie in bed waiting for sleep, I realize something that hadn't registered even as I stood before it. Amid the scents and sounds of Eva's kitchen: the vision of my mother holding a cigarette. She's back to smoking.

Max would be impressed.

* * *

The next morning I find myself up again at near sunrise, blackout curtains be damned. I shimmy into a pair of track pants, a tank top, and flip-flops, tuck a trashy paperback under my elbow, and wander with a buck or two down to the coffee bar just off the lobby.

I'm curled up on a stiff leather couch, two chapters in and halfway through a diesel-fueled *café con leche*, when I notice a shadow across the pages.

"Must be good."

My father nudges me and settles himself next to me on the couch. He's referring to my book, can see that the spine is cracked open down the middle. "Didn't you just start that yesterday?"

I check my watch: 10:03 a.m. How have I lost track of time? How has my father, who regards travel as a competitive sport, let me? Nothing gives him greater pleasure than shearing twelve minutes off an ETA.

"I'm sorry," I say. "It'll take me, like, three seconds to pack. I promise." This is not strictly true, but I can always forgo the blow dryer, just this once.

"Don't worry," he says. "There's no need to rush."

"Who are you and what have you done with my father?" I quip, poking at his ribs.

When he doesn't smile, I go quiet. Something's up.

"What's the deal?"

He sighs and runs his fingers across the top of his balding head, registering a tiny look of surprise at how little hair he actually has left. "It's your mother."

I look at him questioningly.

"I'm sure you're aware that she isn't doing that well."

"Her mother died," I point out. "What exactly would 'doing well' mean?"

"This is *your mother* we're talking about," he reminds me. "She of the mighty Palm Pilot and the bottomless cup of coffee. Energy and control."

I nod, thinking about her semi-catatonic state over the past few days. He makes a good point. I remember that she was smoking—practically chain-smoking—yesterday. For the first time in as long as I can remember.

"This whole thing has hit her pretty hard," he says. I'm about to jump in and reiterate that I still don't find her reaction all that strange—death of a parent, etc.—but he takes a breath and plunges on. "She hasn't said much to me—hasn't said much of anything—but I think that after all these years of not having any communication with her mother, or any of her family, this is even more unsettling than it would normally be to someone in her position."

It's a fair enough theory.

"I'm sure it was a head trip for her to see her sisters after so long," I offer.

"It was," my father says. "It was."

I peer at him. He's getting at something here. Dancing around it. The something that he isn't saying lurks between us like a huge, honking white elephant. No, not even. A pink one. Screaming fuchsia. I'm dying for him to just spit it out.

"What?" I ask.

"She's not going back," he says.

I sit up straight in my seat. "What?"

"To the mainland. She's not going back." He sees my confusion, clarifies. "Not just yet. She says she's not ready. She wants to . . . I'm not sure. But she doesn't want to go back right now."

"When?" I ask.

Summer session starts in a week or so, and my mother is not the type to flake. Not on career stuff. "Hear her roar," etc. . . .

"Don't classes start on Tuesday?" I ask.

"Next Tuesday, but that's not the point. She's going to get someone to cover," he says. "She needs to stay here until she sorts some stuff out."

"What, like her mom's will?" I ask.

"No, no, sweetie. Inside stuff. Her own stuff."

My mind reels. *Inside stuff?*

"I expect that she'll be out here for at least a month. Maybe two," my father concludes.

I don't say anything.

After a moment I notice he isn't saying anything either. But he isn't getting up, going back to the room; he isn't telling me to get upstairs and pack . . . he isn't doing much of anything, short of staring at me, sort of wistfully. Weirdly . . .

It hits me. "There's more."

"She's going to stay with Tía Rosa."

I nod. "Go on."

"But like I said, she isn't in great shape, and she hasn't seen her sisters in years. I don't want her here all alone. She needs someone to stay with her." He swallows. "Emily, she needs you. You have to stay here with your mother."

Three

A unt Rosa's house looks different when it's empty. Not bigger, though, like you'd think. Instead it's filled with clutter: big, overstuffed chairs strewn with throw pillows, bright books and school supplies that probably belong to her younger daughters; inexpensive, simple jewelry that might be Lucy's. It's not like Isabelle's house, where the televisions are flat screen and the sofas are sectional. It's not even like my house, where the doorways between rooms are thick and molded. Rosa lives in Río Piedras, which is the primary suburb of San Juan, very middle-class.

Compared to Isabelle and Adrienne, *I'm* middle-class, but thinking about that, making direct comparisons between my home in New York and Rosa's—"*Tía* Rosa," as she has asked me to call her—makes me feel suddenly, inexplicably guilty.

"And our washing machine is in the back, in the room behind the kitchen," Tía Rosa says, finishing up on a grand tour of the place. There is a kitchen, a living room, a den, the basement where Max had sought sweet refuge, and four bedrooms. Four bedrooms seem like a lot until you realize that one belongs to Rosa, who has been on her own since her husband died four years ago; one belongs to Lucy; and one is shared between Lucy's three younger sisters, Pilar, Ana, and Dora.

Lucy's older brother, José, has his own room as well. This hardly seems fair given how little time he spends at home—at least, as far as I've seen, which admittedly isn't that much.

Anyway, he's not home now.

Pilar, who is thirteen, can't seem to bring herself to care about the washer-dryer combo, not that I blame her. Ana and Dora, who are ten and eight, respectively, gaze at their mother with appropriate if practiced admiration.

Lucy stands off to one side. Her hand is on her hip, and she is trying not to pout. I note that she is either not trying all that hard or not succeeding.

"Gloria, you and"—she chokes on my name briefly—"*Emily* will stay in Lucy's room."

"Thanks, Lucy," I say, trying to coax the sourpuss off her

face. "That's really cool of you to share. We don't snore, I promise."

She shrugs. "It doesn't matter. I'm going to stay in the girls' room."

My face must give me away because Tía Rosa quickly jumps in. "Don't worry, *chica*, there's plenty of room. We just wanted to be sure that you and your mother have enough privacy."

Lucy's expression does not change. I don't think she's blinked in, like, twenty minutes. The surface of her eyeballs must be burning.

"Lucy, show them the room," Tía Rosa says.

Dutifully Lucy jerks her head toward us and then shuffles down a short hallway. Pilar and Ana grab at my mother and my suitcases, shooing us away when we offer to take them ourselves. Of course, the bags aren't that heavy—we'd only packed for a weekend. But still, there is something slightly off about seeing my ten-year-old cousin hoisting my belongings for me.

Lucy stops in her doorway. "It's not exactly a *mansion*," she says, edgy.

I peer in.

She's right; it's not. But it's not exactly a shack, either. It's just big enough to house a twin bed, a desk, a bureau, and a bookcase, all in matching white wood. There's a poster on the wall of a *tejano* star I vaguely recognize from Spanish teen mags that our AP teacher uses to "stimulate cultural awareness." There's a calendar of impressionist paintings. June is Degas. There's a stuffed gray Persian kitten on her bed, grinning at us incongruously. The curtains are pink, and the window looks out onto a backyard that contains a small, circular, in-ground pool. The pool is par for the course in Rosa's development, I think.

My biggest concern is the bed. I have no idea how my mother and I are supposed to share it. Neither of us is exactly a sumo wrestler, but, um, twin beds are kind of narrow. I realize, though, that this would not be the ideal time to point this out.

Lucy leads us to the backyard.

"The pool is nice," I say, aiming for "brightly" and missing it badly. My voice squeaks. I sound desperate.

"We can't afford it," Lucy says flatly. "But Papi put it in and now Mami wouldn't dare cover it over." She sniffs, showing us what she thinks of this attitude.

"It must be nice for the evenings, when school is out," my mother says wistfully. She'd always wanted my father to build a pool, but he balked and made noise about the increase in property taxes.

"I work in the evenings," Lucy says abruptly.

This is interesting news. I'd always wanted an after-school job—a discount at Abercrombie seemed like a jackpot to me—but my parents were pretty insistent that nothing get in the way of my schoolwork. "We give you plenty of allowance," they'd point out.

"Where do you work?" I ask, no longer scrambling to make conversation but honestly wanting to know.

There is no reply. After a moment I realize why. I turn to see that Lucy has slipped away, probably before I'd even asked my question.

Hopefully before I'd even asked my question.

"I don't think she heard you, sweetie," my mother says. She reaches out to smooth my hair in a gesture she'd—up until this point—abandoned after I hit adolescence. I duck away from her touch, uncomfortable. She may be right—maybe Lucy hadn't heard me at all—but really, there's no way to tell.

"She heard you."

My mother starts, and I realize that we have company in the form of a smallish, pixie-faced neighbor child leaning challengingly against the tree that separates her backyard from Lucy's. She pushes off from the tree, walks toward us. Her face is tiny, elfin, with enormous brown eyes and razor-sharp cheekbones. She seems very . . . intense.

She stops just in front of me and holds out her hand. "I'm Marisa."

We shake, solemnly. "I'm Emily. This is my mother."

She nods. "You're Lucy's cousin, right?"

"Yes. Did she tell you we were coming to stay for a while?" If Lucy was talking about us, I can only imagine what she would say. . . .

Marisa shrugs. "Nah. You just look like her," she says, and promptly turns, marching off back to her own yard.

* * *

"So you're, like, stuck in Puerto Rico?"

"Mmm-hmm," I say, pacing in small circles around the pool.

I had remained outside after our preliminary tour for a much-needed moment alone. Of course, a moment alone basically consisted of frantically calling Noah, Isabelle, and finally Adrienne, who is the only one who picked up her cell. I explained to her what was going on: Mom freaking out (which, really, I hadn't seen all that much evidence of beyond her newfound chain-smoking). Dad insisting that I stay behind for the *whole summer.* The vaguely unbelievable promises to pack up the remainder of my summer wardrobe and ship it over to me, lest I spend the next six to eight weeks rotating between four pairs of underwear and one set of velour track pants. The Puerto Rican family, all of whom seem to somehow know of Max and me, even though they don't *really* know us. Fried foods the likes of which would make Isabelle faint dead away into her Atkins-friendly fro-yo. Sharing a bedroom with my mother. Sharing a *twin* bed with my mother. Et cetera.

"Wow," Adrienne breathes after my small explosion has subsided.

"I know."

"That sucks." At least she sounds sympathetic. "It's like . . ."

"Like *Fried Green Tomatoes*. Except with tomatillos," I say.

It's an Isabelle line. Adrienne laughs.

"This means there's no way you'll be able to come on the trip."

"Looks that way. Unless you guys wanted to postpone it."

I'm joking, but not.

"I wish we could"—God bless the girl; she actually sounds sincere—"but there's not even a guarantee that you'll be back in six weeks. And we have to leave for orientation in August."

"I know, Ade, I know. I was kidding. I'd never ask you to put your trip off just for me. It's just . . ." I stop before I can lay on an unintentional guilt trip.

"We'll miss you tons," she says, demonstrating exactly what it is that I love about her. "We'll send you a million postcards. It'll be just like you were there."

Well, not quite, I think, but I'm digging on the sentiment at least.

"I left a message for Isabelle," I say. "But you know, if you talk to her first, you can tell her. Let her know how bummed I am."

"Definitely," Ade assures me. "I think she's out shopping with her mom. I'm sure she'll call you later." She laughs again. "At least your cell works down there."

This is true. Unlimited calling. Small miracles and whatever. I contemplate reminding her that Puerto Rico is technically a part of the United States but decide against it because she's being so supportive.

"Did you talk to Noah yet?"

I shake my head, then realize that she can't exactly see this over the phone line. "No. He's not answering. Don't—I mean, you can tell him, but—"

"I won't say anything until you guys talk. You probably want to break it to him yourself."

"Good call," I agree, grateful for her newfound psychic powers.

Or was Adrienne always like this? I can't remember, but suddenly, more than anything, I wish it weren't going to be six whole weeks—at least—before I can see her in person again. I have a vision of her, camped out Indian style on the hood of my car, grande latte in hand and sunglasses pushed to the top of her forehead.

This is as close as I've come to homesickness in a while. And I've been in Puerto Rico—what? Four days?

". . . know what you guys are going to do?"

She's asked me a question while I've been out in la-la land. *Did you guys talk at all? Do you know what you guys are going to do?*

She means me and Noah. Like, what we're going to do over the summer. Which strikes me as funny. We didn't know what we were going to do even before any of this happened.

Before my grandmother and Puerto Rico.

Now . . .

"Um, not really. Not yet. I won't be home until August," I say. "And he's going to Northeastern next year. . ."

. . . *which is miles away from Brown.* The unspoken portion of my thought lingers in my brain unpleasantly, causing my stomach to dip and flutter.

"It'll work out," Adrienne says. "One way or the other." Which is true enough but not exactly comforting.

"¡Emily! ¡Necesitamos poner la mesa para la cena!" Tía Rosa's voice breaks through the evening air with enough force to shatter glass. I flinch.

"One sec," I call out.

"Who is that?" Adrienne asks, dubious.

"My aunt. She wants me . . . " I think back to her words for a moment. "She wants me to help set the table for dinner."

"She sounds cranky."

"You think?" I ask rhetorically.

We exchange our good-byes and I hang up, face flushed and feeling guilty. Rosa does sound cranky, for real. Unnecessarily so. I have no idea why she would be, but I'm guessing I'm about to find out.

When I hang up the phone, Marisa, Rosa's next-door neighbor, is in front of me again. She stares at me. It's a little bit creepy.

"You better get inside," she says. "We do things differently down here."

I have a feeling she's not wrong about that.

* * *

"Mira, chica, los platos," Tía Rosa says, nodding toward a stack of plates laid out on the counter. I've barely stepped in from outside before she's pointing, gesturing, and offering up orders in rapid-fire Spanish.

Pilar mans a steaming pot of something or other at the stove top while Dora dries wet silverware from the dish rack and lays it out on the table, spaced into individual place settings. Ana is slicing up a loaf of bread. Lucy raises her eyebrows at me and pours water into glasses. There is a routine in place here, and I get the distinct feeling it's Not Okay to be outside on one's cell when others are preparing for dinner.

Not that anybody told me so.

I pick up the plates and set them out in between Dora's forks and knives. Quickly I count the number of settings in my head. "José's eating with us?" I guess.

José isn't here, hasn't been here all day.

Lucy shrugs. "*No sé.* Maybe."

My stack of plates distributed, I lean back against the counter. I don't want to be underfoot, but sitting down feels like the wrong thing right now. "Is there anything else I can do?"

Rosa whirls around from the sink, where she's rinsing vegetables. "There's always something else to do," she says. She shakes her head at me, and I feel useless. "Come here."

She reaches up over her head into a cabinet and pulls out a wooden cutting board. *"Para la ensalada,"* she says, and slides the board, some red peppers, and a knife down the counter at me.

I dig into one of the peppers, overcome with a powerful craving for Chinese. Is this my mother's idea of therapy? Forced labor?

"This is how we do things here," Rosa says, breaking into my thoughts with frightening insight. "I don't know what it is like in your house, but here, my girls help me.

And while you are here, you are one of my girls too. So you will help. You'll be a good Puerto Rican girl before you know it."

Lucy snorts. Loudly.

Rosa either doesn't hear Lucy or—more likely—chooses to ignore her. I wish beyond measure that my mother were here, in the room right now, to hear Rosa predict my future as a "good Puerto Rican girl." The words don't exactly have a feminist ring to them. I surprise myself by laughing out loud.

Rosa sees me laughing, chuckles. "You think that's funny, *mami?*" she asks. "Okay, *sí*, so you're not exactly a *puertor-riqueña*. But you can't deny what's inside."

"She's a *nuyorican*," Dora shrieks, a crazy grin on her little face. "Like you said the other day."

"That's true, *m'ija*," Rosa agrees. She finally puts down her wet dish towel, regards me. "A *nuyorican* and, as I say, one of my girls."

I can live with that, I think, *for six weeks.*

Then I see it—the look on her face that says that we're done with the warm and fuzzy part of the talk and on to something a little more hard-core.

"And Emilia, Esperanza, whatever we will call you for while you're here—"

I blink. Can't she just call me Emily? Do I need to be *renamed*?

"—I must tell you that my girls know my house rules."

I have a sinking feeling that the house rules are, shall we say, extensive. "Well, shoot. Let me have them," I say, then immediately worry that she thinks I'm being flippant.

"We all help to keep this house running," Rosa says. "That includes cooking, cleaning, and watching over the younger girls."

Pitching in at meals seems perfectly reasonable, seeing as how I essentially ousted Lucy from her room.

Cleaning? Well, we have a housekeeper back home who comes once a week, but it's not like I don't know how to run the spin cycle on the washing machine. Mostly.

"Sure," I say. "Of course."

"School is finished now, but the girls are taking summer study courses through our church."

Bible camp? Yikes. I mean, the only time my family goes to synagogue is the high holidays. And, I suppose, at my bat mitzvah. But that was, like, five years ago.

"Okay," I say, not sure how this affects me.

"Lucy will be at work most days. The girls would normally walk *a las tiendas*—to the mall—after camp to meet her and she would walk them home. But this is better. This way you can walk them home."

This probably means that I'm not exactly free to do as I please during the days. And that I will need to get a map of the city.

"Unless your mother is around. You two can work that out together. I think she is going to rent a car."

Big sigh of relief. A car, aka freedom: check.

"On weeknights we eat at seven. The girls know this. I prepare the food in the mornings so that when they get home, they can begin the cooking."

None of this sounds terrible, especially with the wheels factored in. But she's not done.

"After dinner Pilar and Lucy can show you how to clean the kitchen. We mop every other day. Otherwise, the bugs." She shudders. "We wash dishes immediately after we eat."

"Laundry is *por los domingos*, on the Sundays, and *el mercado* is Saturday. *La tele* is only after dinner and only for an hour. Church is Sunday mornings, but you and your mother can decide if you would like to join us there."

Church? Um . . .

"Curfew is eleven on weeknights, midnight on weekends."

Curfew? Wait. What?

I haven't had a curfew in, well, ever. I just . . . come home when things are over. This is unbelievable.

Not that I have anywhere to go, but that could change. Right?

Mercifully the front door bursts open, putting an end to Rosa's Rules and Regulations for *Nuyorican* Living. José saunters into the kitchen.

"Hola, Mamá," he says, striding across the room and kissing Rosa on the cheek.

"Hola, muchacho. Ai, estamos comiendo ahora."

"No puedo. Tengo que encontrar a Carlos a las películas."

Rosa shrugs. She points to the pot that Pilar still dutifully stirs. *"Por favor.* Eat something. *Algo pequeño?"*

He leans over, pulls the spoon away from Pilar, scoops up what I now see is a rice-and-bean concoction. "Mmmm. *Gracias,"* he says. He disappears toward his room. "Gonna grab my jacket."

"Leave his plate in case he wants to eat something when he gets back," Rosa says, to no one in particular. "And go call your mother. We're ready to eat, the rest of us."

"I think she's reading in the bedroom," Ana offers. "I'll get her."

Ana calls my mother, and we settle at the table. Lucy serves the rice and beans and Pilar sets out the salad. After a moment of contented chewing—I totally heart complex carbohydrates—we hear the door slam again. *"¡Hasta luego!"*

Apparently there are way different ground rules for Puerto Rican boys.

Lucy chases a black bean across her plate and onto her fork. She chews thoughtfully. If she's got an opinion about the state of the union in the household, she sure isn't sharing it.

But it's probably just as well.

Later, after dinner, Lucy washes dishes and I dry. I think of our dishwasher at home—which always seems to miraculously load and unload itself—and vow then and there never again to take it for granted.

But drying itself is quiet, automatic, Zen. I focus on the task and not on the fact that Lucy hasn't said one word more to me than is absolutely necessary.

I'm not sure exactly what she has against me. I mean, there's the whole being-kicked-out-of-her-room thing, but still. She's had a chip on her shoulder about me from moment one. And as teenage girls go, I'm a pretty inoffensive specimen. Forgettable? Maybe. That's the flip side of inoffensive. But it's better than the alternative. I have no idea what's up Lucy's butt.

Abruptly she turns the faucet off. The utter silence is deafening. I can hear myself swallow. "Done?"

She nods. "Do you want to go out?"

I'm so shocked, I think I actually physically recoil. "Um, what?"

"Tonight," she says flatly. "Do you want to meet up with some of my friends?" The look on her face tells me exactly how thrilled she is at the prospect. "We're going to a café."

Clearly Rosa put her up to this. It's the only explanation. And given how pissy Lucy's been with me since I got here, the whole idea sounds less than enticing.

Declining, however, is not an option.

"Sure." I groan. I cough and try to muster some genuine enthusiasm. "Sure!"

"Great," she says. She looks me up and down. My jeans are covered in wet splotches from where I leaned the dishes up against them as I dried. "I'm going to change."

She pads off toward her bedroom, leaving me to ponder her subtle hint. As of this very moment, I have exactly two tank tops and a hot pink Juicy hoodie to my name. I will not exactly be knocking them dead at the local Starbucks. But that's okay. My expectations for this evening are appropriately low.

It's just self-preservation. I mean, six weeks? Under certain circumstances, six weeks could be a lifetime.

And this here, this little stint in the motherland, is starting to feel like some pretty certain circumstances to me.

Four

"Where's the café?" I ask, patting the wet splotches on my jeans as if that will help them to dry more quickly.

Lucy signals, peers over her shoulder, and smoothly pulls the car into a minuscule parking spot. So she's an expert parallel parker on top of everything else? Fabulous. Not intimidating at all.

"Um, is that it?" I ask, deciding to assume that she hadn't heard me the first time rather than the other, more obvious alternative.

Lucy turns to me briefly as she kills the ignition. "No café," she says shortly, stepping outside the car and slamming the door in her wake.

My mouth drops open in confusion. I close it, slide out

of the passenger seat, and lock the door behind myself. Once I'm out, I notice that Lucy is buried inside the car again, digging in the backseat. She fishes out first one, then another open-toed, kitten-heeled silver sandal, which she quickly swaps for the sneakers she was wearing when she left the house. "There is no café," she says. "It's a disco."

"A disco?" I repeat, aware that I sound mildly challenged.

"A salsa club," she says matter-of-factly. She gives a tug on her jeans, and suddenly they sit a full two inches lower on her hip, exposing killer abs. My eye catches on her naval, which sparkles with lavender glitter.

"No way could I get a real piercing, but this is cool," she says, catching me ogling. She shrugs off her jean jacket and I have my first glimpse of her top, which is a tight white off-the-shoulder number. The jacket is crumpled into a ball and tossed onto the backseat as well, banished to the realm of the sneakers.

Lucy rummages in her small denim bag for a moment or two longer. "Yes," she whispers triumphantly, opening her palm to reveal a fistful of silver. In go two dangly beaded earrings. She pulls the elastic out of her hair and now she's a vision in blond, a ringer for a pop princess, her hair tumbling down her shoulders in big shampoo-commercial waves.

"I really wish my jeans were dry," I crack. But that's the least of it. If my outfit—jeans, flip-flops, and a tank top—was boring before, my unfavorable comparison to Lucy has knocked me down a few pegs further. For a moment I wonder if I should just throw a bag over my head and call it a night.

She glances at me and—is it possible?—manages the slightest of smiles. "You'll be fine."

I allow myself a moment to feel slightly more at ease. "I mean, no one's really going to be looking at *you*."

The moment is over.

"So, a salsa club?" I repeat.

This is terrible news. I don't dance. Like, for real don't dance. Not even beer commercial dancing—you know, when everyone's had a few cool frosty ones and then the girls decide to do the cheesy sexy hip shake while mouthing along to eighties music at the top of their lungs.

Yeah, not even that. I'm just way too self-conscious. The tragic irony is that I took ballet, tap, jazz, gymnastics—you name it—for years. But something about an actual freestyle dance floor performance suffuses me with dread. Thankfully Noah feels the same way. I get to seem all understanding, sitting with him on the sidelines during the big Britney-style finales at the school dances.

Ha. Lucy snorts. This seems to be a favored method of

indicating her generally low opinion of me. "Yes, a salsa club. But they serve coffee if you really want some."

"Give me a mocha or give me death," I say weakly. "So, I take it Rosa doesn't know you go dancing?"

"I'm eighteen years old and my curfew is eleven thirty," Lucy points out. "What do you think?"

Fair enough.

"Anyway, my friends and I, we have a system. Wednesday we say we're at the library. Thursday it's the café. Fridays and Saturdays we usually say we're going to the mall. It stays open later, so it's not, like, fishy or anything. As long as we're home in time, no one complains."

"But it's Sunday," I point out.

"Yeah, *mira*, this is the one place that's even open tonight," she agrees. "You got lucky."

Lucky, I think wryly, following as Lucy tosses back her hair and marches down the sidewalk toward a point at the end of the street. She whips out a cell phone that I'm sure is both smaller and pinker than the one she used earlier, to field a phone call from her brother. *"Ay, mira, papi,* I'm with the *nuyorican;* we'll be there in a minute. *Cállate."* She wiggles her hips and the jeans slide down again.

Lucky, lucky me.

* * *

Inside, the club is much smaller than I expected. I'm

not sure whether or not this is a good thing. On the one hand, it's not that overwhelming. On the other, if I were to attempt to dance—or even approximate a reasonable facsimile thereof—there's really no protective camouflage. I put my hands in my pocket, ten kinds of uncomfortable.

Lucy shrieks and clatters forward toward a group of girls huddled against the bar. They shout right back at her and shimmy in her direction. I quickly scan the uniform—jeans or capris. Unlike New York basic black, they're all wearing very tight shirts in bold, bright colors. One girl is wearing white pants.

If the sum contents of my entire wardrobe were dropped at Rosa's doorstep tomorrow, I'd still have it all wrong. Beyond my dark coloring, there will be no blending here.

As if that were ever a question.

I take a deep breath and cross the Spanish tiles to where Lucy and her friends are now huddled. One of them, a short, dark-skinned girl with masses of curly black hair piled in a high ponytail, steps forward. "*Hola*, I'm Pia." She smiles. I do a double take. Yep, she is smiling—at me. Can she really be *Lucy's* friend?

"Hi, I'm Emily," I say. I extend my hand to shake. Pia looks surprised, but she takes it, still grinning. "*Mira*, this is Ramona"—she gestures toward the taller girl with long, straight hair—"and Teresa."

Teresa is so incredibly gorgeous that I don't know if I

can bear to be in the same room with her. She has pin-straight hair so blond it's almost white, and her eyes are Liz Taylor lavender. But she is beaming at me so openly that I can't help but smile back.

"Bienvenida, gringa," she says to me. "Lucy says you're here for the summer?"

"Six weeks," Lucy interjects flatly.

"And you're from New York?" Pia asks.

"Westchester. New York State. It's the suburbs, really. Kind of like this."

"Kind of," Lucy says, her voice thick with what I suspect to be sarcasm. She looks around. "Where are the boys?"

Pia gestures farther down the bar. *"Las cervezas."*

Oh, right. Beer. Cool.

I drink about as often as I smoke. That is to say, never. God, I'm a loser.

No sooner has Lucy asked about "the boys" than a tall, muscular one with close-cropped black hair is leaning over her for a kiss. She obliges, smiling. I can't help but notice that Lucy is really, really pretty when she smiles. I still have no idea what rare form of personality disorder it is that prevents her from smiling at me, but since her friends seem to be immune to it, I can probably get through this night at least.

Bolstered by the warm reception I've gotten from Pia, Ramona, and Teresa, I step toward Lucy's boyfriend. "Hi, I'm Lucy's cousin, Emily," I say.

He nods. "Right. Lucy mentioned you were coming out. Rafael. It's very nice to meet you. *¿Cómo estás?* How are you liking Puerto Rico?"

"It's great," I say, realizing as the words come out that I'm sort of lying. "It's beautiful." That much, at least, is true.

"Yeah, we like it. Bummer excuse for a vacation, though, huh?"

"I, um, didn't really know my grandmother. I mean, I never met her," I stammer, flushing. I'm mortified to realize that I almost forgot why I was here in the first place.

"Quiero bailar," Lucy says, not to me.

Rafael shrugs. "Sure, chica. Ricky's in the bathroom, I think, but he'll be out in a minute." He looks at me questioningly. *"Tú quieres?* You up for some salsa?"

I bite my lip. "You know, not just yet." I try to make it sound like it's just a matter of time before I'm grinding on top of the bar. Like I'll be all *Coyote Ugly* ("but without the bar brawls," my interior Izzy champions) in just a few short moments.

"Are you sure?" Pia asks, sounding genuinely disappointed.

I nod. "Just for now. I'm kind of tired. I'm still, uh, really jet-lagged."

Lucy's friends are kind enough not to point out the

total lack of time difference between New York and Puerto Rico. They scamper toward the dance floor, squealing.

I settle back against the bar, grateful to be out of the spotlight. I watch the girls—and Rafael—dance. It's amazing; they're all ridiculously good. And they're dancing for real, not the sort of hip twitching that passes for dancing in New York clubs. They're actually step-ball-changing forward and back, weaving in and around each other with little cha-cha-cha flourishes and sexy hair tosses (the girls, that is; I mean, Rafael is dancing but without any hair-tossing).

"Well, now, if you're not going to dance, you can't just stand here empty-handed."

A cold bottle of beer is thrust into my hand and I turn. "Oh, um, thanks," I say.

My benefactor is a curly-haired guy with light brown eyes and freckles scattered across his nose. He's wearing a short-sleeved, linen button-down shirt that's one part school nerd, one part refugee from a Fitzgerald novel.

Somehow, though, on him it works.

"Ricky," he says.

"You were in the bathroom," I offer, immediately wishing the ground would open up and swallow me whole. "Rafael said," I finish weakly.

"Well, yes, it's true, but I didn't realize it was my claim to fame."

I laugh, feeling no less moronic but slightly better about it. "Emily," I say.

"The *nuyorican.*"

"Why does everyone keep saying that?" I ask. "It's like you've never met anyone from the mainland before." It feels so good to be talking to someone who is actually talking back that for once I don't seem to have any internal censor.

"Well, you have to know that you're sort of a legend around here," he says. "At least, your family is."

"What?" I'm totally baffled. There is nothing legendary about the Goldbergs. Like, my dad tends to win the annual Woodland Thanksgiving Turkey Trot, but I doubt Ricky would know about that.

"You're the New York family, the family that no one's ever met, not since Gloria left for college. That's a big deal. You're like . . . the Loch Ness Monster. Or Bigfoot."

"Oh, that's a compliment," I tease.

"Well, you're a source of speculation," he says. "Lucy was incredibly curious to meet you."

I must have some sort of involuntary facial twitch because he explodes with laughter. "She's not that bad."

I don't say anything, just struggle to keep my features neutral.

"Her bark is worse than her bite," he finishes.

"It's a pretty loud bark," I say, before I can stop the words from coming out of my mouth. I have to mentally pinch myself, remind myself that he is actually Lucy's friend and therefore probably likes her. Talking trash about her simply will not do.

"Yeah, it's just . . ." He pauses. "Anyway, it's great that you're here."

It's just what? I think. I am dying to know what the end of that sentence was, but he's being so gracious about my indiscretion that I don't want to push.

"Ricky, *baila conmigo!*"

It's Lucy, smiling brightly and beckoning for my new-found ally to join her on the dance floor. Her lips are stretched tightly—too tightly—across her teeth, and I have to momentarily wonder if she's ticked that he and I are being so chummy. It's an ugly, suspicious thought and I push it away.

"You're not going to dance, are you?" he asks me, and I find myself incredibly relieved that he seems to get it.

I shake my head.

"Are you going to be okay over here?"

"Yeah, no problem. You go." I wave him to the dance floor.

"All right. But I'm coming back after one song." He pauses thoughtfully. "Two songs, max."

* * *

We drive home with all of the windows down, Lucy fanning at herself frantically. "Shoot, shoot, my hair reeks," she says fretfully. "*Tengo problema.* I need to quit smoking!" She's usually so self-possessed, seeing her discombobulated is unsettling for me. We turn into her community and she lowers the headlights, gnawing on a fingernail and clutching the steering wheel like Mr. Magoo. She leans forward and peers out the windshield, squinting.

As we approach her house, she sighs. "She's asleep." Meaning Rosa, obviously.

"How can you tell?"

"Her light is off." She points toward Rosa's bedroom window, which is indeed dark. "She doesn't usually wait up, but you never know."

I can*not* get over how different Lucy's life is from my own. I've never, ever had a curfew, which may explain why I can't fathom the idea that she is willing to risk sneaking out, and being caught, night after night.

She pulls into the driveway and kills the ignition. Now I panic, praying that the noise from the car doesn't wake Rosa.

"We're going in the back," Lucy whispers. "That way we don't have to walk past her bedroom."

She leads me through the fence and into the backyard. We tiptoe to the door off the kitchen. Lucy's got this down to a science, I see. She slides the key into the door and rattles it just so, pushes the door open just enough to squeeze herself in. After I'm through, she gently guides it back into the door frame. I'm impressed; this is some serious stealth. She takes off her shoes and motions for me to do the same. At this moment I allow myself the thought that Lucy and I are partners in crime, accomplices—especially what with how we've gotten away with it. But then Lucy turns to me shortly and mouths simply, "Good night," and pads off to her room.

I sigh. I make my way carefully to my bedroom—Lucy's bedroom, of course. I would love to talk to my mother about this, to whine about curfews just to hear what she has to say on the subject, but she's out cold when I get to the room, sleeping in a tight coil against the wall, leaving space for me even from the deep recesses of REM stage. I sigh and feel around in the semi-dark for my pajamas.

The real truth is that if Mom were in any shape to talk about things like curfews and clubbing, then we wouldn't even be here to begin with.

Five

Y ou guys—do you think we should spend one day at Yellowstone or two?"

It's Adrienne, hunched over a road map in concentration. We're sitting in a generic motel room, standard orange pattern bedspread and sailboat seascape paintings in place. Adrienne sits cross-legged on the one bed; Isabelle is upright next to her, legs stretched out in front.

"Two, for sure," Isabelle says. "I mean, Yellowstone?"

I shake my head. We want to hike most of the trails as much as we can, and we want to spend some time at the geysers too. Even allotting two days, I'm thinking we'll be rushed. But I don't say anything. I never say anything in situations like these. Why is that?

I open my mouth. "I just think—" I stop.

Words that had formed so clearly in my mind are now
stuck, a mental hiccup. I can't remember at all what I was
going to say.

* * *

I sit straight up, heart thudding dully in my chest. The
sheets are twisted underneath me, my shorts ridden up and
sticky with sweat. *What?* I reach my left arm across my body
to grab at my alarm clock and am surprised when my fingertips scrape against the wall instead. I run my fingers
through my hair.

It was a dream, of course. Isabelle and Adrienne are back
in Westchester. They leave—for Yellowstone, among other
places—sometime this week. I think Wednesday. I idly
wonder how much time they ultimately decided to allot to
that leg of the adventure.

Me, I'm still in Puerto Rico—tropical temperatures,
spotty air-conditioning. Tía Rosa's house is equipped
with the modern amenities, but climate control in Lucy's
room comes in the form of a ceiling fan that traces lazy
circles above me, stirring the humidity rather than allevi-
ating it. God, if I'm hating this room as much as I am,
with the heat and the two to a bed, I can only imagine
what it's like for Lucy, stuffed in across the hall with her
three sisters.

The fact that I'm in bed alone means, obviously, that my
mother has already woken. I trade my pj's for my track

pants and a tank top—that clothing package *needs* to arrive soon—and wander out.

I find my mother at the kitchen table, idly stirring a cup of coffee. "Good morning, sweetie," she says when she sees me, as if on autopilot. "Did you sleep well?"

"Uh-huh." No point in mentioning the dream. If it has any great significance, I can't figure out what it is. I drift to the refrigerator, pull out a carton of orange juice.

"*Ay*, there's a glass set for you at the table."

I nearly jump out of my skin. Tía Rosa is behind me, pointing toward the table and the glass in question.

"Right, thanks." I take a seat.

"*Qué quieres comer?* We have eggs, cereal, toast, bacon. . . ."

"Oh, um . . . I guess cereal's fine," I say. She offers me a veritable buffet, three different choices. I pick the one with the highest sugar content and dig in. "Where's Lucy?" I ask between munches.

"Taking a shower. She has to drive the girls to church. Their summer school starts today."

"I'm so excited!" offers Dora, who I realize now has been sitting patiently at the end of the table. It's pretty cute, actually.

"You're so excited, but you're going to be late if you don't get dressed," Rosa warns.

Dora bounces in her seat. "But I have to . . ." She looks at me, trails off.

Rosa nods. "*No es un problema.* I will do it just this once. Go—you can wear the pink skirt."

This is apparently extra-fabulous news because Dora beams and skips off.

From the direction of the bathroom, I hear the water in the shower turn off. A few moments more and Lucy is in the kitchen, wrapped in a robe, her hair piled high in a terry-cloth turban. "I got it, Mamá. You can go."

"*Gracias.* I have work, then." She turns to my mother. "You'll be okay?"

"Of course, Rosa. We have the grocery list, so Emily and I will take care of that. We might as well make ourselves useful. You've been so generous in taking us in for the summer."

Rosa is quiet for a beat. Then, "Of course." She grabs her keys, shouts her good-byes to everyone—"Tell José dinner at seven"—and is off.

Lucy hovers over me. I tap my spoon against the bottom of my cereal bowl, unsure of what she wants. "Can I . . . do something?" I ask.

"No, it's just, I have to clear the table when you're through."

"Oh," I say awkwardly. So she's been waiting for me. "*Oh.* I'm almost—"

"No rush." She cuts me off. "I'll just load *the dishwasher* once you've eaten."

It hits me more fully: Dora was covering for Lucy while she showered; Rosa was covering for Dora while she dressed. And now Lucy's waiting. For me. I'm not sure about this. On the one hand, they could have just told me to rinse my dish when I was done.

On the other, I'm horrified to realize that it wouldn't have otherwise occurred to me.

* * *

Lucy insists on taking her sisters to church camp herself, but my mother decides she wants to tail her. "This way we'll be able to do it on our own eventually."

We dress quickly and head out to the car. "Couldn't we, like, just get directions when the time comes?" I ask.

It's not that I have anything better to do today. Mom's got a grocery list and some errands to run. (Being this close to the beach and knowing that I'll be spending my afternoon at the dry cleaner's is torture.) But one look at Mom's face—deep lines and grayish pallor not improved by chain-smoking—and I decide to keep my gripes to myself.

She's actually laughing now.

"Directions?" Apparently this is pee-in-your-pants hilarious.

"What?" I ask. "I don't get it."

"That's because you've never driven in Puerto Rico, sweetie. Directions are useless. You either know the way or you don't. Haven't you noticed that there aren't really any street signs around?"

"Well, I haven't been driving myself," I point out, easing into the passenger's seat.

"No, I guess you haven't," my mother allows. "Anyway, the thing is, if you're from around here, you know the main roads, and you can sort of feel your way from there. But otherwise you're screwed."

I start back, my seat belt snapping as I twist.

Screwed? Not typical language for Professor Goldberg. But I don't say anything.

"So if we're going to be here and get around, we have to feel our own way. I'm sure it will come back to me eventually—some things you just don't lose—but for now, tailing. At least until the main roads become second nature again."

"A lot has probably changed, though, right?" I ask. "I mean, the roads can't be exactly the same."

My mother becomes quiet for a moment, wistful. "They haven't changed that much."

I sense that there's more meaning in what she's saying than she's ready to share.

* * *

We follow Lucy as she takes the girls to church camp. It's not far from us, though my mother is completely right. Puerto Ricans drive like maniacs. No one has heard of a turn signal, and street signs are totally nonexistent. Technically my New York license is valid here, but by day three I've sworn to myself that I will never get behind the wheel on my own. It seems to me that I have two choices: one, to remain on good terms with my mother and join her on her cultural renaissance or whatever she's doing here, or two, to forge blindly forward in a friendship with Lucy who has, up until this point at least, demonstrated the type of interest in me that one might feel toward a new strain of toenail fungus.

To Lucy, I'm a curiosity and not necessarily a welcome one. I'm an *interloper* and utterly housebound at that.

I suppose these two choices are not necessarily mutually exclusive. But they are equally dependant on some rather specific action. And I'm just not the type to take action.

I don't think.

* * *

The next few days pass quickly. The language barrier keeps me on my toes, and I can't help but wonder again what the deal is with those AP classes and placement exams. *Qué tiempo hace*, my ass. The *tiempo* is always the same in Puerto Rico: sunny, with a light breeze and little humidity. If it rains, it's only in intermittent pockets, and it never lasts.

By now I wake up on time, on my own. Even as an early riser, I find I'm the last person up—but at least now I'm in the ballpark. I come to breakfast to find Lucy, Pilar, Dora, and Ana gathered. But they're not waiting for me anymore, so that, at least, is something.

Their routine is well choreographed. Rosa is up first,

before dawn even, and she gets breakfast ready. Once the girls are awake and settled with their breakfasts, she's off to get ready for work, a day shift as a nurse's aide at the local hospital. From there Lucy takes over: she makes sure the younger girls eat, reminds them to clear their places, and then washes up after them. Pilar helps Ana and Dora dress. And so forth.

Mom and I eat with the girls. We don't take over their self-appointed chores or tasks because that would disrupt the delicate balance that they've created. But we have taken on our own roles. We run the daytime errands, taking clothing to the cleaners, bringing appliances in for repair, and, most frequently, bringing home groceries for dinner. I still refuse to drive, but by the end of my second week I could find my way to the supermercado and back blindfolded. We do the laundry, to which I am contributing more now that my father has sent along some clothing. We start preparing dinner at five. By five thirty my mother goes to pick up the girls at camp. Lucy and Rosa are home, along with the girls, by six. By six thirty we eat. Sometimes José joins us. Sometimes he doesn't. I don't ask. Lucy mentions his girlfriend, a freshman at the local university. But she doesn't live in the dorm, so I have no idea where they spend their time.

The younger girls clear the dinner plates and head off to do their "homework" for camp. I have never attended a camp that required homework, but since it mostly seems to involve a lot of coloring, what do I know? Lucy disappears at night, usually to her room. I imagine she's talking on the phone to Rafael, Pia, Ramona, Teresa, or maybe even Ricky. Seeing as how he was so genuinely nice to me, it makes sense that I think about him sometimes. Since he's Lucy's territory, though, thinking is as far as it goes.

I miss talking on the phone at night. But Isabelle and Adrienne are away by now, and it's catch-as-catch-can. As for Noah . . . well, he never answers his phone, and I'm starting to wonder what it was we always talked about anyway.

Lucy and I haven't had a night at the "coffeehouse" since my first Sunday in Puerto Rico, which by now feels like it was ages ago. Sometimes there's a *telenovela* hour where we all gather around the television in the living room and I pretend to understand what the bosomy actresses are getting at as they wave their fingers and squeeze tears from heavily made-up eyes.

I think of asking my mother about the beach again or if maybe there isn't something else to be seen in Puerto Rico. But she's distracted, doing a lot of concentrated staring, so I settle for laps around the tiny pool and wondering what leg of their ride Izzy and Ade have hit. I'd call, but . . .

Well, I'd call, but I don't.

* * *

"You hate it here."

It's been long enough that I've become fairly accustomed to Marisa's sneak attack visits. I don't know what she does all day in her house—but it may or may not involve spying, as it were, on me. She tends to emerge whenever I've just gotten comfortable, either on a lounge chair or on a raft in the pool itself.

Today I'm perched on that same lounge chair, *Us Weekly* cracked open but facedown on my stomach. I'm not so much on the dieting habits of supermodels just now. The day is bright but not sunny, and I'm soaking in the UV rays.

I wonder how you say *ultraviolet* in Spanish?

"You hate it here," she repeats. She squints at me behind bug-eyed sunglasses. She's channeling La Lohan or an Olsen twin, with the oversized glasses and a ruffly pink dress that's at least three sizes too big.

"What?" I have the distinct impression that I'm being put in my place. By a fourth grader. Somewhere along the way, my life has veered horribly off course. Or at least my summer has. I should jump in the pool, duck underwater, and refuse to come up again until Marisa's gone home. But it's too late; obviously she's already seen me.

I'm not sure quite what to say in response to Marisa. *Hate* is a very strong word, as they say . . . yet not entirely inaccurate. I am not overcome with affection for this place, that's for sure. I miss my friends, my brother, my father, the mother I had before all this started. My boyfriend . . . or the idea of my boyfriend—if only he would take my calls. I might be more open toward Lucy if only she showed the slightest modicum of interest in me.

"No, I don't."

She raises one eyebrow at me. I'm *totally* getting grilled by a ten-year-old. Wow.

"Well, there's not all that much going on," I admit. I actually feel guilty about admitting this to Marisa. I've stumbled into an alternate reality.

"There might be."

"Might be what?"

"Might be more going on." She points to my lounge chair. "If you maybe left the house."

I peer at her disdainfully, then realize . . . she's right.

"You could be on to something," I admit reluctantly. "But there's . . . you know . . ." I wave my magazine at her feebly.

She cracks a grin, pulls up her own lounge chair. Carefully, with great purpose, she plucks off her sunglasses and pulls her dress over her head, revealing a polka-dotted bathing suit. She positions herself just so on her chair, next to me.

"How come you don't hang out with Rosa's daughters?" I ask.

She wrinkles her forehead. "They're always at Bible camp."

True.

She reaches over, swipes my magazine. "Who's splitting up this week?" She sighs and settles in.

* * *

After Marisa has returned to her house, I'm struck with a burst of inspiration. This is Puerto Rico. It's a Caribbean island. It's the origin of my misplaced cultural heritage. Somewhere in the recesses of my suitcase is a guidebook. I should Get Out. See Something.

But I refuse to drive by myself.

I head into the house to find my mother. Maybe this will be it, our opportunity to bond. She'll overcome whatever emotional trauma has recently been dredged up. We'll rediscover ourselves.

It will be like *The Joy Luck Club*, except in Spanish.

I find my mother in our bedroom, sound asleep. I check my watch: 1:30.

I don't think Rosa would approve. Which is probably why my mother is taking her nap *now*, when we're alone.

I sigh. The Spanish Joy Luck Club will have to wait.

* * *

Max, my wonderful, intuitive brother, surprised me, dropped a present in my package from my father. He wrapped it in my favorite pink terry-cloth pants, knowing that then there'd be no way for me to miss it—*Siddhartha*. A small, battered copy that I know for a fact he bought for two dollars at a used-book fair on the Lower East Side. It's his favorite book and a prized possession; my throat caught involuntarily when I found it grazing my J. Crew wedge espadrilles.

The book is dense, and it doesn't help that this copy looks like it spent a few years underwater before being blow-dried back to its normal state. I leave it lying on the nightstand in the bedroom for a few days, feeling guilt-ridden at my lack of appreciation for what was obviously a very personal gift. The guilt doesn't make me want to read it any more urgently, though. It's not until Tuesday night, when yet another dream of home wakes me, that I reluctantly slide out of bed, grab for it, and pad silently out of the bedroom and into the living room.

Siddhartha had it pretty good, I can tell. He was a sort-of hottie, and the back cover copy says that he had a "promising future." I think I can relate. But he gave it up for a journey of spiritual enlightenment. Is Max trying to tell me something? From where I sit, spiritual enlightenment sounds way overrated.

A noise from the kitchen startles me. Before I can wonder what it is, though, I turn and see Lucy, shoes in hand, creeping in. She stops when she sees me.

My mouth drops open, but she holds a finger to her lips just in time, reminding me to keep it down. *Where have you been?* is my unspoken question, but she gets it.

"With Rafael," she whispers. "We had coffee."

I raise an eyebrow.

"We had coffee," she repeats. "Sometimes we really do that."

"Was it fun?" I ask.

"Yeah," she says, but she shrugs noncommittally and her body language suggests otherwise. I'm too overcome with surprise for this to really register, though. Obviously this isn't the first time I've seen Lucy sneak into the house, but for some reason, I just assumed . . . I don't know, I guess I assumed that when we all went to bed, she did too. It's one thing to blow curfew, but another entirely to sneak out altogether. My mind races; how many nights has she done this? For all I know, she's been out every night since I've arrived. I'm far too impressed to be offended at the thought of her partying without me.

"I won't say anything," I promise. She shrugs again. This girl has apathy down to an art form.

The knob to the front door turns and the door opens. Now José walks in, though without any of the covertness of Lucy's arrival. But I have had my quota of shock for the night and Lucy, of course, could care less. *"Hola,"* he says, not bothering to whisper. He looks at Lucy. "You were out?"

"Rafael," she says.

He nods. "I'll be around tomorrow, but I'm sleeping in," he says, and wanders off to his bedroom.

"I guess that means we can set an extra place at the table," I quip after he's gone.

Lucy's not amused. She glances at her watch. "I have to get to bed," she says, sighing.

"I can drive the girls tomorrow," I offer. "That way you can sleep a little bit later." The words are out of my mouth before I can register what I'm saying.

Lucy shakes her head. "I have to start breakfast, get them dressed. . . . Thanks, but there's too much to do."

"Seriously, I can take care of it. I've got your routine down," I say.

Lucy finally appears to be considering my proposal. "Do you really know where the church camp is?"

"My mother can find it," I say. "From that day when we tailed you."

Lucy shakes her head again, this time a quick, decisive *no*. "Mamá would be upset," she says, more to herself than to me, even. She heads off to her room, pausing briefly.

"Thanks, though. *Muchas gracias.*"

"*De nada,*" I whisper to the empty room.

Six

Wednesday morning starts off like any other: Lucy is up moments after Rosa, fussing over the girls and helping with breakfast. Since I know what time she went to bed last night, I'm even more impressed than usual; her energy is limitless even without taking that into consideration. She's slightly cranky, the only sign that something might be up. But then again, I can't remember the last time she was actively friendly to me, so cranky isn't exactly a far cry.

I poke at a bowl of cereal, and Dora shows my mother her latest church camp masterpiece, a watercolor self-portrait that is, I must say, a pretty accurate rendition, all things considered. My mother smiles halfheartedly at the painting—most of her movements these days are halfhearted at best—and offers up her typical promise to have dinner ready by six.

My mother, who at home keeps the local Chinese place on speed dial, is now the self-appointed Guardian of Dinner. Puerto Rico has had a strange effect on her.

Once everyone's left, the house feels empty. You'd think I'd be excited to have some space to myself for once, but instead it's like a Yiddish parable come to life: the rabbi tells the poor man to cram as many of his barnyard animals into his shack as he can; once he removes them again, the place feels shiny, new, spacious. I could roller-skate from room to room if I wanted.

The Yiddish parable connection is a weird one, what with where I am and all. Also, the thing is, I haven't studied any of that stuff since my bat mitzvah. "Jewish" is like a default state of being, whether you are conscious of it or not.

I glance at my watch. Nine thirty. The dishes are done and nestled in the drying rack. Grocery shopping is my only "to do." Maybe I'll pay a call to my good friend Siddhartha. He seemed to make do, in his story, with just the basics. Maybe I could pick up some pointers from him.

I'm on my way into the bedroom when I bump into José.

I totally forgot that he even came home last night. What is it with this place? In such close quarters, you'd think you'd be on top of everyone's coming and going, but instead it's a crapshoot who's even home. Crazy. He's wearing a towel, clearly off to take a shower, and I'm mortified.

"Uh, hi," I stammer. "Sorry."

"You're here," he says, making it a statement rather than a question. I'm not sure how to respond; clearly he knows my mother and I are staying for the summer, right? And if he doesn't, it's *definitely* not my place to tell him.

I nod. "Yeah."

"What do you do while everyone's out?" he asks, as though the question has just occurred to him. Which, come to think of it, it probably has.

"Errands," I say. "We start dinner."

"That takes you all day?" he asks incredulously.

"Not really," I admit. "I was going to read."

He shakes his head. "*Mira*, I know your mother is sort of out of it these days"—understatement—"but you're in Puerto Rico. I'm guessing folks back from your hometown come here for vacation, *sí*? Fun in the sun?"

"Right, but . . ." How to put this . . . "Things are pretty . . . messed up."

"Your mom hasn't been here in years," José points out. "She's staying for a reason, and it isn't just to help my mother with dinner."

I can hardly argue with that.

He purses his lips, appears to be considering something very deeply. "I'm not working today."

José works? I have literally not a clue what the boy does with his days—or his nights, for that matter—and we're technically living under the same roof.

"Have you been to Old San Juan?" he asks.

I shake my head. "I don't know how to get there," I say, as if that's the only reason, or even the primary reason, that I've yet to visit.

He laughs. "You're missing the point. I do."

* * *

Once José is dressed, he hunts my mother down in the backyard, where she is enjoying her first cigarette of the day. He breaks his brilliant plan to her without, I admiringly note, even a moment's hesitation.

I expect her to beg off, and at first it looks like she's not too keen—kind of waving her hands in a wishy-washy way—but inexplicably he's insistent and charming, and the next thing I know, we're piled into his car, me sitting shotgun, off to Old San Juan with José as our tour guide.

José has a *car*?

"I bought it myself with the money from my first job," he says, slightly bragging but all in all very matter-of-fact. "I mean, a chunk of the paychecks go to the house, *por supuesto*, but I took on enough extra shifts because I knew I would need a car. The same with Lucy."

Por supuesto. How many T-shirts would I have to fold at the Gap in order to pay for my own car?

"I haven't seen it in the driveway," I hedge.

"I haven't been home," José agrees. But he doesn't offer anything more as to where he spends his time, so I don't ask. Now at least I know that he has a girlfriend (if only because Lucy has mentioned it in passing) and a job. That's, like, two hundred percent more than I knew about him this time last week. A twenty-one-year-old boy with a job and a girlfriend might not be around that often, I guess.

"You're at school at the local university?" my mom chimes in from the backseat. I'm flabbergasted; I guess this means she gets the scoop from Rosa? Not that that's so strange; it's just I've never felt so disconnected.

It occurs to me that if there's something I need to know, maybe I should just ask. What a novel concept.

"Two more years," José confirms. "A year and a half if this summer session goes right."

Another clue in the mystery of José's schedule slides into place.

"Is Lucy going to go to the University of Puerto Rico too?" I ask, emboldened. This may be my only chance to get the dirt on Lucy without having to be subjected to her full-force sarcastic scowling. She is, like, an Olympic contender in disdain.

"Lucy?" José bursts out laughing. Seriously, he's laughing so hard he's wiping tears from the corners of his eyes. I can't think of one reason why my question would elicit this kind of response.

"Are you kidding? You think she'd spend one minute more than she has to on this island?" he asks once the chortling has subsided.

I shrug; well, clearly not. Funny, I had figured she was dying to graduate high school and marry Rafael. Not from anything she'd said outright . . . it was just something I'd . . . assumed.

He spells it out, just in case his maniacal laughter left any room for doubt. "She does what she has to do, you know, to help Mamá, but once it's time for college, she's out of here. She wants to go to New York."

"Really? But . . . what about Rafael?" I ask. I don't know Lucy all that well, but I can't imagine her leaving town without him.

"I'm sure she wouldn't mind if he went with her," José explains. "But for her, New York is the priority. She has a scholarship to NYU, and that's where she's going to be."

I take it in silently as the scenery slips by in a stream of colored blur. I've learned more about Lucy and José in the past two hours than I have in the past week plus, total.

It's a lot to think about.

And here it is, not even noon.

* * *

El Morro, as it turns out, is one of two forts remaining of the original city of Old San Juan. Back in the 1500s, San Juan was a walled city; El Morro protected it against sea attacks. Or so the brochure tells me. It's linked to its less-famous land-facing brother fortress, San Cristóbal. We examine a scale model replica of the layout, trenches, dried-out moats, and endless stucco expanses.

Without the model I might not grasp the scope of the city, but small clay figurines don't do justice to the view over the crumbling walls. I don't think it occurred to me before today that Puerto Rico has an actual history of its own.

It's downright hot, for a change, and we're exposed. There's no shade to be found against the flagstone pavement. I squint out at the ocean, the sunlight glittering against the water. José has disappeared.

A shadow falls across my shoulder and I turn to find my mother, also peering out at the landscape, cupping one palm over her eyes to shield against the sun. "It's pretty, isn't it?" she asks absently.

"It's old," I say. What I mean is, *it's older than I realized,* but that's not how it comes out.

Thankfully—but not surprisingly—she doesn't bat an eyelash. Doesn't seem to register anything at all lately. "Yes." She sighs. "They settled this fort in 1540. San Juan was founded in 1519. But none of this was preserved until the sixties. And then in the eighties it was declared a World Heritage Site."

Okay . . .

My mother's area of expertise, to the best of my knowledge, is women's studies. I had no idea she was an authority on the history of Puerto Rico too.

"It's a wide wall," I observe, because it is. I saw the scale model, of course, but now that I stand in front of it, it towers above me, threatens to devour me. It's solid, powerful, overwhelming. It's crackling in the heat of the sun, as I imagine it has been for so many centuries. "Keeps things nice and . . . contained." What am I even talking about?

Inexplicably my mother leans forward, hugs me toward her fiercely. Ow.

"It goes both ways," she says mysteriously.

"Right." I think for a moment, then frown. "What?"

"The wall, Em. It contains things, sure, but isn't it . . . mostly . . . keeping things out?"

Well, sure. I thought that was the whole point of a wall. Is there anything wrong with that?

I notice that my mother is grinning. This may be the most animated that I've seen her since we've come to Puerto Rico.

The Great Wall Epiphany has been good for her.

I myself am more confused than ever.

* * *

When I get home, I check my cell phone to find a text message waiting for me. WON BIG ON THE GAME. MISS YOU.

Noah, obviously. A text message from Noah and I

missed it. More than that, I have no idea what game he's talking about. I'm spending the afternoon with my mother, who's babbling cryptically about good fences and yadda yadda, and meanwhile I'm so disconnected from my boyfriend that he's off male bonding and I know nothing about it. I have stumbled into a Spanish-speaking wormhole in the time-space continuum.

This tiny, seven-word message gives me a palpable ache in my throat, my stomach. Back home, Noah and I spoke every day. Obviously we saw each other in school, but there were phone conversations, IMs, and countless text messages beyond that. Since I got here, we've been playing phone tag. Being apart sucks. It's that simple. And I don't know how much more time I'm going to have with Noah before we both go off to college. This could be it for us.

Could have been *it for us,* I correct myself. It's done, after all. I'm here for the summer, reconnecting with my mother and helping her to reconnect with . . . God knows what. And suddenly I'm more than confused. I'm annoyed and resentful.

I slip out to the backyard, settling into a lawn chair. I punch Noah's key on my speed dial, noting that my breath has quickened. I'm nervous?

"What's up, this is Noah. I'm not around, but leave a message . . ."

I check my watch again. Six. Deep down, I know there

are any number of things he could be doing that would be totally legitimate, but I let my mind run rampant anyway. He could be out with his friends at a movie, babysitting his younger brothers, running an errand for his mother, sure, but it feels more satisfying to imagine him on a date. After all, there's no Ade or Izzy around to rat him out. He could get away with it scot-free. Who would it be?

Hmmm . . . I fixate on the petite blonde who sat in front of us in chemistry last year: Angela, I think her name was. Angela Haring. She totally had the hots for him.

Never mind that as far as I know, Noah has never, ever dated a blonde.

Never mind that he's supposed to be *my* boyfriend. The pity train has already left the station.

I hang up without leaving a message.

"Bad news?"

I nearly flip backward in my seat, I'm so startled. I look up to find Lucy's friend Ricky grinning down on me. He's wearing a short-sleeve T-shirt over a long-sleeve T-shirt and manages to look like a refugee from the Hispanic OC. I drop my phone, scramble to retrieve it. "No, um, just a . . . you know, voice mail."

"You look really . . . bummed." With his accent, *bummed* comes out sounding cute, actually.

I hastily try to rearrange my features into a more neutral

expression. "No. Nope." I can see by the look on his face that he isn't buying it.

"I'm disappointed." I sigh. "I haven't been able to get in touch with my boyfriend."

That sounds pathetic.

"I mean, he has a job and he's out a lot."

That sounds even *more* pathetic. I seriously need to quit while I'm . . . well, not ahead, exactly, but before I shoot my entire foot off. "Anyway . . ."

"You wanted to talk to him," Ricky says reasonably. "Your boyfriend."

"Yes," I agree. "But he isn't around." I try to change the topic again. "Anyway, what are *you* doing here?"

That sounds dreadful, like an accusation.

He laughs, showing a broad smile and even, white teeth. He doesn't seem remotely bothered by my total lack of social graces. "I came to say hi."

I raise an eyebrow. "Lucy's not home yet."

"I've known Lucy since grade school, *chica*, you think I don't know her schedule?"

Fair enough. But that still doesn't explain why Ricky would have come by. Unless he's here to . . . see *me*?

"Lucy's been in her own world lately anyway," he says, almost to himself.

It hits me: she hasn't been out salsa dancing while I sit and rot in her former bedroom. She's been spending one-on-one time with Rafael . . . just like she said. That's something. I'm still not sure what, but she's evidently been blowing off Ricky as much as she has me.

Um . . . yay?

"So," Ricky says, as if reading my mind and choosing to disregard my less-appealing thoughts, "I'll talk to her eventually. But I wanted to see how you were doing."

I shrug. "I'm fine. We're keeping busy."

"Making dinner?"

I smile. "It's a routine."

"You're definitely the kind of girl who lives for routine."

I can't tell if he's being sarcastic and, if he is, whether or not that would be a compliment.

"Anyway," he continues, before I have a chance to respond. "I was thinking we should break up your routine. I mean, you deserve to have some fun while you're here, right?"

"I went to Old San Juan today," I say, almost by way of protest.

"Do you want to go to the beach on Saturday?" he asks, wisely choosing to ignore me.

"What? Oh, sure," I say, stumbling over my words. "With you?"

I can't get anything right this evening.

He chuckles again. "Yes, with me. But not just me. I mean, I was thinking we could get the group together. Lucy and her friends. Rafael. We do that a lot, on the weekends, that is. So you should do that too, with us. Give you an idea of how the locals live."

"I thought only the tourists go to the beach," I say.

He shakes his head emphatically. "They go to a different beach, yeah. But we love it in the water—it's fun, and it's cheap."

"Sounds perfect," I say, because suddenly it really, truly does.

"Great," he says, looking really, truly thrilled at the prospect. Is he actually that concerned with my enjoyment factor?

"Are you sure Lucy's free?"

"Saturday afternoons are the *only* time that Lucy *is* free," he assures me. "It's been that way since the beginning of time."

"Well, I'm sure she'll want to spend her one free hour a week with me," I snark. The words are out of me before I realize they've even crossed my mind. I would never have said them aloud if I'd had a minute to think.

To his credit, Ricky's still laughing. I must say, he has a very nice laugh. Very sincere and not at all patronizing.

"You should give her a chance, Emily," he says, and it gives me a little tingle, the way he pronounces my name. *Emeelee*—as if it were a Spanish word inherently. "She'll surprise you. Like I told you, she's not as bad as she seems."

He leaves, promising to be in touch before Saturday. I find myself incredibly intrigued to see how Lucy is going to take this development. I have the distinct feeling that she will not be pleased. But then, it wasn't exactly my idea, now, was it? And anyway, Ricky told me to give her a chance. He said she'd surprise me. And he really seemed to mean it.

Maybe he's right. The island is full of surprises, after all. I mean, here I am going to the beach with a bunch of *puertorriqueños* on Saturday at their own invitation. And to tell the truth, I'm pretty excited about it.

Full of surprises indeed.

thought this place was a big tourist trap."

I sit sprawled on an oversized beach towel that my father had the forethought to include in my care package. I'm glad I don't have to ask Lucy for a towel. It's best not to have to ask too much of Lucy.

So far this afternoon she has tolerated me quietly, but it's plain to see that she is *un*thrilled to be baby-sitting me on the one day a week she gets to hang with her friends.

I remember that when she came home Wednesday night and found Ricky and me setting the dinner table together, her eyes narrowed into tiny catlike slits as she forced her lips into a grin.

"*Bueno.* Isla Verde, what a good idea," she murmured when Ricky suggested the beach.

"Yeah, it's a big tourist spot because of all of the hotels,"

Ramona says, back in the here and now. She flips through an issue of Spanish *Cosmo* idly, for all the world a dead ringer for Isabelle's languid weekend disaffect. From where we sit on the beach, I can see the hotel that I stayed in when we first arrived. The guests sun themselves on oversized bleached beach chairs and sip at brightly colored drinks with thick, twirly straws. It's a whole different planet up where they are, separated from the plebes by a sun-washed wooden tanning deck and heated swimming pool. At the moment, though, I don't mind the galaxy that I've stumbled into.

"When we go ourselves, we usually go to Condado," Pia chimes in. "It's quieter there. That's where people from our school usually . . . chill." She hesitates on the last word as though trying out the slang. There aren't too many deviations between their English and ours—they watch the same TV, after all—but now and again I've noticed Lucy and her friends get self-conscious. Which is funny. I mean, half the time when they're speaking in Spanish, I've got no idea what they're talking about anyway. It's not like I'm going to judge.

But back to the matter at hand, which is that Ricky specifically took me to the touristy beach, when all along I had thought he wanted me to feel more, um, *authentic*. So much for not being thought of as the token gringa. "But"— I glance at Ricky—"I thought you wanted me to have the real Puerto Rico experience."

Ricky flushes. "Condado is too quiet. This place is more of a scene."

"And I seem like the kind of person who would prefer a scene?" I giggle involuntarily, surprising myself. I am not, as a rule, a giggler.

"*Sí, mami,*" Rafael says, winking at me and letting Ricky off the hook. "You're obviously a wild woman." Lucy glares at him. It's quick, but I don't miss it.

"I prefer this beach anyway, and we never get to come here," she says, shaking her head so her hair fans out over her shoulders.

I'm not terribly surprised. Lucy *does* strike me as the type who would prefer a scene. "Family from the mainland *never* comes to visit."

What can I say? I'm not sure, but for some reason I feel slightly guilty.

"The tourists always have the best swimsuits." Ramona sighs and nods at me. She may or may not be compensating for Lucy's seething hatred.

I look down at my suit, a simple two-piece from J. Crew in a deep shade of eggplant purple. As a representative of the tourist faction, I'm letting my people down, big time.

"Purple is my favorite color," Ramona continues, practically reading my mind.

"Mine too," I say. We settle into silence for a moment.

Lucy exchanges furtive glances with Rafael, once again giving me the urge to giggle uncontrollably. Things in the group are definitely askew. But I'm too tired, too weirded out, and frankly way too nonconfrontational to figure out how to make it better. If nothing else, at least Lucy's friends are being nice. And we have the same taste in crappy reading materials, I've learned.

"Does anyone want to read this?" I wave the trashy magazine I've been skimming through. I'm embarrassed to admit that miles away from home, I still need my weekly gossip fix. *Entertainment Weekly, In Touch, People, Us Weekly* . . . I'm like a junkie. Somewhere deep within my straw tote *Siddhartha* sits, all but abandoned. He would not have approved of Cameron Diaz's shopping habits, I don't think. Or mine either, I'm sure.

"Who's on the cover?" Teresa asks, curious. It's a blond starlet, someone to whom Teresa actually bears a startling resemblance. She wrinkles her nose in distaste. "Ugh, I hate her. Ever since she had an affair with that actor. The one that was married." She shudders, which makes me laugh. I mean, that sort of thing is pretty par for the course, at least according to *In Touch.*

"Oh, come on," I argue. "Not like she was the first. Besides, doesn't he take any of the blame?" Now I'm in familiar territory. I warm to the subject, feeling more comfortable than I have in days. "I mean, *he* was the one that was married, after all."

"That's the way it goes, though." It's Lucy now, her tone flat. "It's the woman's responsibility to behave. The boys can do whatever they want and no one says a word."

Our little group goes quiet for a moment. She's right, on some level—maybe more so in Puerto Rico than on the mainland. Here machismo is the order of the day—so yeah, I get where she's coming from. Still, there's a quality to her tone, something about the look on her face that makes me nervous. Something that makes me think this is more than idle conversation. Rafael just rolls his eyes.

"It's the old double standard," I say, trying to lighten the mood. "It's been going on for centuries."

Lucy sighs loudly.

"I'm thirsty," Pia says abruptly. If it's an effort to change the subject, it's not too subtle, but I'll take it.

"Me too," I jump in quickly. "Who wants a soda?"

Pia, Teresa, and Ramona all eagerly voice their assent; various orders for diet drinks are tossed out. Rafael shakes his head, a quiet "no."

I raise an eyebrow at Ricky. He stands, brushes the sand off his legs. "No. I mean, yes, I'm thirsty, but you don't have to bring me anything." He stops, takes a breath. "I mean, I'll come with you."

Ricky's behavior is uncharacteristically awkward, which I find oddly endearing. I chalk it up to the weird vibe that Rafael and Lucy are putting out. We're all trying aggressively not to notice them. In my whole life, I've never not noticed something as hard as I am not noticing this.

"Sure," I say. I shake my hair out, pin it back up off my neck. One thing, at least—I'll be heading back to Westchester with a killer tan. They'll think I'm a *puertorriqueña* for sure. Even if they're the only ones. I grab my wallet from my bag, extend my arm, beckoning to Ricky. "Come on."

* * *

Once we're alone, I exhale deeply. "What is going on back there?"

Ricky shrugs. *"No sé."* He looks uncomfortable. I get it: Lucy is his good friend. There's a fine line between filling me in and dishing. You don't dish about your good friend. I respect that.

We walk along quietly. My flip-flops make a slapping sound against the pavement. There's no boardwalk here: either you're staying in one of the luxury hotels, or you're a local making your way down the cigarette-studded sidewalk. Tourists have spas and swim-up bars; locals have Taco Bell. It doesn't take too long to figure that out. We duck into one quickly and load up on soft drinks. Ricky carries them in a cardboard caddy, cradling the tray against his chest.

"She's been out with Rafael a lot lately," I offer. It's sort of a last-ditch effort to get to the semi-bottom of this. I'm not totally sure what the point is of trying to talk to Ricky about Lucy, but Lucy seems unhappy, and that affects me. In more ways than just the obvious.

"I guess they're going through some stuff," he says.

I think back to the sound of Noah's voice mail. He hasn't called me back. I haven't texted him back. He's so far away right now. It's hard, and then, it's also . . . not so hard.

"Relationships are difficult," I say. "And Lucy seems . . . like a challenge." I wonder if I've gone too far in the direction of insulting her.

Ricky half snorts, half chuckles. "*Sí*, you could say that." He pauses, shifts the tray of sodas again. The damp cardboard bisects a dark pattern across the center of his T-shirt. "But not as tough as you think. You should cut her a break."

I shoot him a look. "Trust me, I'm trying." He looks disappointed, and instantly I feel bad. "But I'll try harder."

It's not just for Ricky that I say this, I realize. It's a pact that I make with myself too. I have to try harder with Lucy or the next few weeks will be a nightmare. My intentions are totally noble. I just hope that I'm able to live up to them.

* * *

When we return to our spot on the beach, Lucy is lying

on her towel, on her back with one arm flung protectively over her eyes. She is wearing her headphones, and a tinny techno beat blasts from the earbuds. It sounds as loud as if I were wearing the headphones myself. That can't be good for her. Rafael's back is turned to her; he's hunched over a Game Boy and seems totally engrossed. Pia, Ramona, and Teresa continue in the tradition of overcompensating for the butter-thick tension that blankets the air.

"Ooh!" Pia leaps up and squeals as though her Diet Sprite is the best gift she's ever gotten, hands down. It's cute, though forced. She downs half of it in one gulp.

Teresa has read the article about her doppelganger starlet; we spend the next half hour or so discussing upcoming movies that we're dying to see. Puerto Rico is behind us on releases, but not by much. I score some extra points by revealing carefully plotted spoilers for some of the bigger impending blockbusters. Ricky is impressed to learn that I've seen some honest-to-God movie stars in Manhattan; I think it's pretty cool myself but remind him that having dinner at the table next to Tom Cruise is not *exactly* the same thing as having dinner *with* Tom Cruise. It's nice, though, to feel glamorous. Back home, Izzy has a Jude Law sighting that trumps my own. Of course.

When the alarm on my sports watch sounds, I'm startled. It's five. We've been at the beach all afternoon. It's been ages since I've given any thought to sunscreen. Not good. But nothing to do about it now.

I nudge Lucy gingerly, unsure whether or not she's asleep. There's no reply, and there's no subtle way to handle this since her music is still blasting full force. I prod her slightly less gingerly. She removes her arm from across her eyes and slowly peels her eyelids open, peering at me suspiciously. *"¿Qué?"*

"It's five," I say apologetically, pointing to the face of my watch as if she required proof of this fact.

She shrugs, clearly unimpressed with my ability to tell time.

"We have to pick up Ana and Pilar from their playdate," I say.

We promised Rosa. Dora has a music lesson, but the other girls need transport. One condition of our afternoon off was that we come back in time to get them before dinner. Around here there are always conditions.

This seems to register. She grabs at her shorts, shimmies into them, shrugs on a tank top, twists her hair into a bun. "Are you guys ready?" she asks her friends, all of whom readily agree. Rafael looks reluctant to power off the Game Boy, but after a pointed beat, he does. He zips it into a protective case lovingly.

Ricky shoulders my bag, holds out my sweatshirt for me

to slip into. The gesture smacks of boyfriendliness. Yet it doesn't feel totally wrong.

Interesting. And also slightly unsettling. I make a note to revisit this line of thought later, when I've had some time to recover from the sun. Right now I'm definitely a little bit woozy. I do let him carry the bag, though. It's the type of gesture that generally eluded Noah when we were in a group, and I'll be honest, it's kind of nice. Ricky laughs, a quick, easy laugh, and I feel self-conscious, worried that my semi-inappropriate thoughts are etched across my face. "What?"

He shakes his head. "It's just funny."

I glare at him teasingly. "What's funny?"

"That you would be the one to remember when it's time to go home."

I can't help but crack a smile. "You know me," I say. "I love a good routine."

"*Vámonos,*" Lucy says, breaking into the moment. "We're going to be late."

We won't, of course, because as Ricky pointed out, I got us going. But I decide not to say as much, just for now. For now I just bite my lip to keep from grinning too widely.

* * *

When we get home, Marisa is sitting on the front steps of her house. She's holding a coloring book but not actually coloring in it, more sort of staring off into space and humming a top-forty tune to herself. Do they have TRL in Puerto Rico? She jumps up when she sees us. She hugs Lucy, whose maternal instincts kick in as she squeezes Marisa back. I guess it's from all of those years as de facto caretaker. Max and I are nothing like Lucy and her sisters. I can't remember the last time we hugged each other.

Marisa doesn't hug me. Rather, once she's disengaged from her embrace with Lucy, she looks me up and down. "You got tan," she says.

"Yup." I nod.

"You look like you had a good day."

For a moment she looks like she's considering hugging me. I stiffen. The moment passes.

And she's right, of course. Just as usual. It was a pretty good day.

* * *

After dinner I'm surprised to find a voice mail from Noah on my phone. When did he call? How did I miss it? It kills me that my reception is so iffy here. It's not like I can camp out on my bed sitting stock-still, just waiting for the phone to ring. I mean, I *could*, but that would be lame.

"Hey, babe, it's me. Just got back from a Yankees game—we lost, which sucks—and thinking of you. Isabelle and Ade e-mailed; I guess they found a cybercafé somewhere outside of DC? But you know all that, I'm sure. Anyway, gimme a call."

They found a cybercafé? I'd know all that? Noah is assuming that they e-mailed me, of course. Which maybe they did. But Rosa doesn't have the Internet in her house.

It looks like I'm going to have to search out my very own cybercafé if I want to communicate with my friends this summer. I frown at my cell phone.

"Ooh, was that your *boyfriend*?" Dora leaps out at me from behind the bathroom door, wrapped in a towel and wet hair clinging damply to her shoulders.

I jump back, then recover. She's giggling maniacally, delirious with hysteria at the thought of me having a romance.

Yeah, yeah, my failing long-distance relationship is a big old laff riot. "Yes," I admit. "It was."

"What did he say? That he wants to *kiss* you?" She shrieks at her own cleverness and dashes down the hall to her bedroom before I have a chance to answer.

I wish that was what he said.

"Dora! Put on your pajamas before Mamá gets upset!" It's Lucy, shouting forcefully from inside their overcrowded room. I hear a *thump thump thump* that may or may not be Dora bouncing on top of her bed. For her sake, I hope she's not. Max was never like this; I have no idea how Lucy copes. The worst he ever did was keep me up all night plucking angsty notes on his guitar.

My brother, the tortured soul.

"Are you going to call Rafael?" Dora croons, warming to her favored subject of the evening. Her voice reverberates even through the closed door. "Are you going to call and tell him that you want to *kiss* him?"

More muffled shouting and ambient noise. Then, "*Mira*, if you don't get off the bed, you're not going to dinner at Eva's tomorrow!"

That seems to do the trick. Silence. Then the door swings open again, and Dora pads back to the bathroom. "I have to brush my teeth," she explains as she passes me. She looks thoughtful. "Lucy doesn't want to talk about Rafael tonight." She lowers her voice to a whisper. "I think they had a fight."

She scampers away before I have a chance to respond, but the thing is, I think she's right. And I have no idea what, if anything, to do about it.

* * *

The last thing that I want to do is confront Lucy about her argument with Rafael. I kind of like my head and prefer to have it actually attached to my body. But . . .

I guess I know what it's like to be unsure about your feelings for someone. I certainly have no idea what's going on with my boyfriend. And the truth of the matter is that if I had to guess, I would say that Lucy is much more attached to Rafael than I am to Noah.

Just a hunch, seeing as how it's becoming clear to me that

most of my feelings for Noah are more about the idea of Noah than Noah himself. I mean, seeing as how we've yet to have an actual conversation since I got here.

I knock on Lucy's bedroom door, let myself in without waiting for an answer. She's braiding Ana's hair. "Come in," she snaps, peeved at my intrusion.

"Hi," I say, feeling awkward, like my arms are four times too long for my body. "Are you . . . okay?" I'm not sure what I even mean by this, but I can't think of another way to pose the question.

"I'm fine." She shrugs. "What do you care?"

"Well, I just meant that if you want to talk . . . about anything . . ."

"With you?" she asks, as though I am clinically insane. As though I've just suggested that she confide in the tiny colony of unicorns living in my belt buckle.

This is the most I've put myself out there in ages. And it hasn't exactly gone smoothly. What's the next step? Damned if I know. I open my mouth, think for a minute, close it again.

I leave the room without saying anything more.

Eight

On Sunday we all have dinner at Tía Eva's. I learn that this is a relatively frequent post-church activity: Lucy and her sisters head to a late-afternoon mass, then bring a dish of something or other over to their aunt's.

I've been to a mass once before, when Adrienne's grandfather died. I have no problems whatsoever being in church, though I'm never totally sure what to do when everyone else is kneeling. My favorite thing about the service is that it only lasts an hour or so. Anyone who has ever been to synagogue on Saturday morning knows that this is, by comparison, a breeze. If synagogue service lasted only an hour, heck, I'd go every weekend. Maybe.

Anyway, mass in Spanish is pretty, though the language is flowery and even harder than usual to understand. Dora,

Pilar, and Ana all sing in the choir, and they are very cute standing up in front of the chapel. I've heard them practice around the house, but it's different with the full backing, the organ, the whole shebang. Lucy smiles at them appreciatively from beside me in the pews. Even José is here, freshly shaven and showered, scowling and detachment kept to a minimum. He's okay, I've decided, though he definitely marches to his own rhythm. Rosa plays the organ and beams at her girls. My mother chants the hymns quietly but surely to herself, making me wonder what else from her childhood she's retained but never shared.

We split up afterward, my mother, Rosa, and the girls in one car, José, Lucy, and me in the other. I almost can't believe he's coming with us to Eva's, but then I remember that he's friendly with her sons, Carlos and Juan.

Eva and her husband, Héctor, live in Bayamón, a large metro area just southwest of San Juan. It's a quick drive that José obviously knows well. The car ride is quiet. I stiffly balance a pot of rice on my knees that clanks dangerously every time we turn a corner.

"So, what did you think of church?" José says, teasing. I know he thinks being Jewish is something tantamount to being an alien.

I shrug. I don't get the way some people are all uncomfortable around religions other than their own. It's not as though just sitting in church calls my entire religious identity into question, after all. Or at least, it shouldn't. "It's not the first time I've been to mass."

"You were there for Grandma's funeral," Lucy says, and again—again—I want to protest that in fact, my grandmother's not dead.

And then I remember. And I can't believe it because, of course, I got it wrong. Again.

Eva and Héctor's house is big, bigger than Rosa's. It's also in a development, which I'm realizing is standard for most middle-class families. Héctor is "in business," though I'm not really sure what that means. He used to work with Rosa's husband, before Rosa's husband died. This also is pretty common, the whole tight-knit family thing. Living together, working together.

I think of my father's family back in New York, grinning at each other through tightly clenched teeth and clutching at their highballs. The idea of them all working together is enough to make me snort with laughter.

I think about sharing this with my mother; she's in the kitchen, of course, hunched over a pot of something or other. I think she'd appreciate it, but maybe not right now.

There's melee here, but not quite at the level of the post-funeral chaos at Rosa's when we first arrived. Still, the house is clogged with people, and only a handful are faces that I recognize.

Carlos, Juan, and José immediately disappear into someone's bedroom to talk sports or whatever it is that teenage boys do behind closed doors (I honestly couldn't even guess). Dora, Ana, and Pilar head off to play computer games with three other little girls vaguely within their age bracket. I have no idea who these girls belong to. Amalia fusses in the living room, setting up a communal buffet. I stand awkwardly in the living room, shifting my weight from one leg to the other. I should be doing something helpful, but what? The kids don't need looking after. Amalia has got the table covered all on her own. The kitchen is overflowing with bodies. I suppose I could, um, vacuum or something, but that seems like more of a post-party, cleanup thing.

"You are Gloria's daughter, *sí*?" A man with the weathered face of a raisin leans in, reaches out to pinch my cheek. It's all I can do not to jump. Families are all the same, I guess, with the in-your-face-ness and the awkward vibes. Huh.

"*Sí*, er—yes," I reply. "That's me."

"She doesn't speak Spanish," Lucy interrupts, which, while technically true enough, doesn't really apply in this instance. So, whatever.

"Tú te pareces exactamente como tu mamá," he continues. He's either totally ignoring Lucy or his English is about as good as my Spanish. He's also speaking in that super-slow way that some people do when they think it will help you to understand a foreign language. But I get the gist—I look like my mother. It's true, I'm sure, but suddenly the information carries with it new meaning.

"That's what they say," I offer lightly, hoping he can get my point from context. Lucy raises an eyebrow, possibly impressed that I've scaled the language barrier. Possibly. With her, it's so tough to tell.

"Your mom is in the kitchen," Lucy says, in such a way that makes it clear that I should be there with her. There is, however, a little less bark to her bite.

I shove through the crowd—at least there's no cigarette smoke yet (a concession to the Sabbath?)—to find my mother at the stove. She's dropping chunks of something floured into a hissing, spitting pan. "What are you making?"

"What? Oh, there you are." She smiles at me. *"Bacalao.* Salt cod."

Barf. Fish sticks are inauspicious regardless of geography. Also, my mother's most famous dinner is her Monday night phone call to the local Italian place. What is she thinking, actually cooking something?

"Salt cod?" It's out of my mouth before it occurs to me that I might be insulting, oh, everyone here.

"It's Spanish originally," she explains. "You take the cod—filet, of course—"

"Of course—" I tease. I mean, that much, at least, I got.

She ignores me. "And you soak it. It can be for a few hours or overnight. But you soak it in salt water so it takes the flavor."

Fair enough. I have nothing against sodium.

"And then you dredge it in flour—"

I gesture to the big honking pile of damp flour that's spread on the countertop next to her; yes, *I understand.*

"And you deep-fry it."

"Very, um, health conscious," I say, as though I've never eaten, like, a bacon double cheeseburger.

She hands a chunk of freshly battered fish to me. It's still warm. "Try it."

I do. My suspicion erodes the moment the food touches my lips. The crust is just crisp enough without being overly greasy. The fish inside is delicate, more subtle than I would have thought, tangy and flaky.

"Like a fancy fish stick," I quip, my initial thought validated. "Very South Beach friendly. Not."

But Mom can see through the comment, I know. The fish is delicious.

"Yeah, señorita, you have to watch yourself," my aunt Amalia says, grabbing at her own ample glutes. "You've got the *puertorriqueño* genes, and so . . ." She smacks her own backside again for good measure.

She's not slapping *my* ass, but I'm mortified just the same. Is she implying that I'm fat? Or that I'm *destined* to be fat? Is she right? I've been lucky enough that I don't have to worry too much about what I eat, but . . .

I catch the twinkle in my mom's eyes, recall her frowning, squinting dance in the Century 21 dressing room every bathing suit season.

Destiny, genetics, who cares? I'm fine, and anyway, it's funny. I laugh. So does my mother.

"*Mira*, if you're so worried about health food, you can help me," Rosa says.

My mother shoots Rosa a quick look, then glances back at me. She hasn't interfered with the curfew and the house rules at Rosa's, of course—when in Rome— but she does care, she does want to be sure I'm not *totally* losing my mind here, abiding by Rosa's helpful "guidelines" and "suggestions."

"What are you making?" I'm worried.

"*Arroz con gandules*. Rice and beans."

"Rice and pigeon peas," my mother corrects her. "That's what they are, technically. The type of beans. Very healthy. Carbs."

I contemplate giving my mom a refresher course on the basics of the South Beach principle. But then, I don't really care right now.

"It's my mother's recipe," Rosa says.

"*Our* mother's recipe," my mother says. She's all about precision this evening. Rosa ignores her.

"I'd love to learn how to make it," I hear myself say. Not only that, but as I say it, I realize, I mean it.

"You think the *bacalao* was bad for you?" Lucy chimes in. "This is going to be fun." For once she doesn't sound like she's being sarcastic. This in and of itself is momentous. Sign me up for rice and beans, then, stat.

"How horrible could it be?" I ask. "You've got your rice, you've got your beans. I mean, simple carbs, sure, but no big."

I've been eating a lot of rice and beans since I got to Puerto Rico. I'd say it's my favorite of the local dishes. And I have a sneaking suspicion that I'm about to learn why it tastes so much better here than plain old rice has ever tasted in the mainland. I'm going to learn, and then, possibly, I'm going to regret it.

Lucy grins fiendishly. "There's a secret ingredient."

She reaches into a cabinet just below the sink and pulls out an oversized industrial tub, which she sets down on the counter with a resounding thud.

"What is that?" I squeak.

She waits, then—"Lard."

Oh. My. God.

I giggle. What else is there to do? Lard, clearly, is a very delicious substance. Who knew?

I turn to Lucy, roll up my sleeves. "Fine. Lard. Bring it on."

I am *so* relieved, not for the first time since I've gotten here, that I am not a picky eater.

"Come here," my mother says, patting her leg in a gesture intended to call me over to her side. "I'll show you."

* * *

We return home in a carbtastic, lard-smeared post-meal coma, José shaking his head ruefully as Lucy and I belt out the words to the latest top-forty song on the car radio. Seriously, processed animal fat has done wonders to bring us together. I don't even care that my waistband is digging into my stomach. Together Rosa, my mother, Lucy, and I cooked enough rice to feed an army, which was just the right amount for the whole extended family.

After dinner chairs were cleared out of the dining room and salsa music was cranked up. Lucy and her mom busted into an impromptu rendition of dance fever, which roused everyone else from their food stupors. I don't know whether or not it was typical post-church behavior, but everyone really seemed to enjoy it. Including my mother, who wove eagerly back and forth across the makeshift dance floor, grinning at me, beckoning.

I am sorry to say that I didn't get it together to join her, but I was stunned to find myself giving it thought. *Serious* thought. Puzzling, but I decided to chalk it up to the carbs.

José smoothly pulls into the driveway. "I'm off to see Angela," he says.

"Your girlfriend?" I ask, feeling more familiar with him than I have since I'd arrived.

"Of course," he says. "I never told you her name?"

I shake my head. "Believe it or not."

"He hides her from us. He's ashamed of her," Lucy says. It's hard to tell whether or not she's kidding, she's so deadpan all the time. But since we've had a fun night, I decide to give her the benefit of the doubt.

"*Ay, mami*, it's not her I'm ashamed of," he says. He winks to take the edge off his words. She rolls her eyes. Really, they're not so different from Max and me.

As we approach the house, the door opens and my mother emerges. She, Rosa, and the girls must have broken every speed limit on the way home. Or I guess Rosa drives like a true *puertorriqueña*. Mom's waving something at me with some urgency. As I move closer, I can see that it's her cell phone. "Your father," she says.

I know she talks to him every few days, but he's so busy that I don't get much more than a minute or two here and there myself. I wonder what's up. It's Max's birthday next week, Thursday—but it's only Sunday, so it's not as though I've messed up yet. I take the phone from her, cross the threshold into the foyer. "Hello?"

"Hi, Princess!"

It's not until I hear my father's voice that I realize how much I've missed him. I shake my head, willing the lump in my throat to dissolve. "How are you?"

"We miss you, babe, but things are good here. Max has been practicing his guitar, I've been at work or else at the club"—my father is *very* into his golf—"but otherwise, nothing special. The house is quiet with you and your mother both gone."

"I'll bet," I say. It's not all that quiet down here, but I don't point that out.

"So your mom sounds like she's doing well," he says. He wants affirmation, I can see.

"Oh, yeah, she's having a good time with her sisters, and we're sightseeing and relaxing," I tell him, leaving out the part where she's suddenly a massive chain-smoking chimney. "Today I learned to make rice and beans. Just don't ask me what the secret ingredient is," I warn. "Hearing it would give you a heart attack."

He laughs. "Okay, enough said. But listen, this conversation is costing a fortune, and there's a reason that I called."

My ears perk up. "What?"

"Well, I'm sure you know that it's Max's birthday on Thursday."

"Of course." I've already mailed him a snow globe of a scene from *el centro* and a stuffed *coquí*, the small frog native to the Puerto Rican rain forest. We have a running gag on out-tacky-ing each other when it comes to birthday gifts, and I'm pretty sure I've got a lock on this year. Mom paid for the super-fancy postage.

"Well, you've been such a good sport about staying down in Puerto Rico with your mother—"

I have?

"—and I know you gave up a lot this summer in doing so—"

I sure did

"—so Max and I wanted to let you know . . . well, if you'd like to come home for his birthday, we'd be—I'd be happy to pay for it."

This was not what I had been expecting. *At all.* "Does Mom know?"

"Yes, I already talked about it with her and she thinks it's a great idea. She would totally support it. It's just

Wednesday through Saturday, after all."

I'm quiet for a beat, so quiet that my father chimes in again. "Princess? What do you think?"

What do I think? Hallelujah is what I think! This is my reward for going to church on Sunday! (Except I'm Jewish, so not really. Or maybe it's some sort of weird reverse reward. But whatever. *Not the point.*)

I could go home, sleep in my own bed, eat frozen yogurt from my favorite place, watch bad TV on our TiVo. I could *freeze-frame bad TV on our TiVo.* I could go for a run around my favorite park. I could poke Max in the cheek while he's trying to study.

I could call Noah.

"That's . . ."

And then it hits me.

It's a great offer, a thoughtful, incredibly generous offer. But . . .

Wednesday's soon. Like, three days away soon. And my mother . . . I glance into the kitchen, where my mother is nursing a cup of coffee—decaf, I hope—and chatting with her sister. They're both smoking, but they seem relaxed. My mother's doing better, seems to be coping with her own mother's death, but she needs . . . something. I'm still not sure what. But it has something to do with being here and with me. With being here *with* me.

Then again, Noah is at home. Do I want to see Noah? It's not even a question.

"That's what?" my father prods.

I realize I've been quiet for a few moments too long. "That's . . . amazing," I tell him. "Thank you so much. But, um, can I think about it?"

"Sure! Of course. Though I have to admit, I'm surprised. I thought you'd jump at the chance to spend a few days back here."

So did I.

"Yeah, but Mom is . . ."

Mom is smiling and talking animatedly at this very minute. It's genuine, and it's really nice to see.

"Do I have to decide right this second?" *Please say I don't. It's too tempting, and I really don't know.*

"No, no. You have until tomorrow. The ticket is on reserve. You just need to either cancel it or confirm it within twenty-four hours of the flight, which is Tuesday evening. But don't stress about it, kid. Whatever you decide will be fine. We'd love to have you, but Max won't be offended if you stay down there."

"More cake for him," I say.

"Exactly. Do you have a pen? Let me give you the number for the airline and all the info you'll need. Just let me know tomorrow what you decide."

I take down the information, a string of numbers and letters that when woven together represent freedom, a brief respite, a temporary get-out-of-jail-free card. I promise him I'll call him tomorrow and let him know what I decide. It should be a no-brainer. Four days at home. Duh. It should be easy.

It *should* be, but it's not.

Nine

D*ear Noah—*

What's up?
Long time no speak.
Sorry I missed all of your voice mails and text messages
. . . and that you missed mine—

[delete]

Hey, Noah—

Where have you been?

[delete]

Noah—

So, I know you were freaked out about me bailing this summer to "reconnect with my cultural roots," but the truth is that in some weird, freaky way, it's been good for me—

[delete]

It's Monday, and José has driven me to a local Internet café. I'm *thrilled* to discover that in fact, I haven't gotten a single e-mail from Noah.

Out of sight, out of mind?

Okay, not totally fair. I mean, we've been playing a mean phone-and-text tag that is as much my fault as his. He does call. I do hear his voice mails. Yet . . .

Yahoo mocks me. *You have 0 new messages.*

I could put an end to this. I could take my father up on his offer—for a thousand reasons that have nothing to do with Noah, even. And then I could see him.

I wouldn't be going home "because" of him. And I'd have other obligations while I was there. In certain ways, it would be the perfect solution.

Mom wouldn't mind at all. She's doing much better; gardening with Rosa and playing board games with the girls at night. Smoking slightly less. She'd be fine, and anyway, I'd only be gone for a few days.

Lucy would want me to go, I'm sure of that. In no uncertain terms. No one in that house would mind having a little bit more space, even for a short time.

"What are you going to do?" José asks from the next terminal over.

I'm surprised; I hadn't realized that he had any idea what was going on in my head. "You heard about my dad's offer?"

He nods. "If I were you, I'd want to go home and see my man. I mean, if I were a girl," he adds sheepishly.

I shrug, try not to dissolve into hysteria at the description of Noah as a "man."

Is there something wrong with me that I'm not desperate to see him? We had a good relationship—*have* a good relationship, I remind myself—but it hasn't been too terribly hard to be without him. And there's no denying that the text messages and voice mails lack a certain urgency.

Besides, the girls, Ade and Izzy, are halfway to the Rock and Roll Hall of Fame by now, no?

"It's awkward to break up the summer that way," I say lamely.

"Well, I mean, didn't you already do that? Break up the summer? When you came here?"

Touché. He's right, of course. The whole freaking summer was completely turned on its end. But I still have no idea what to do.

* * *

José drives me to the mall, promising me a "real native Puerto Rican experience." I refrain from pointing out that we have malls aplenty in Westchester. He pulls into the parking lot, kills the ignition. "Anything you need?"

Somehow I don't think I'm going to find it here. Though a pair of white denim capri pants could go a long way toward soothing my soul.

We walk down the halls of the shopping mall, which is vastly different than what I am used to back home. Every third shop is a CD store, a sports store, or a Wet Seal–type clothing store. Payless-style shoe stores line the perimeter as well. Had I known about this place, I could have kept myself in velour track pants, denim skirts, and platforms *all summer long* . . . and for a reasonable price.

Still, I'm glad that my father sent my own clothes to me.

We stop at a Wal-Mart; I buy several huge bags of various types of gummy candy and two celebrity tabloids. My favorite pop singer—pregnant! Good stuff. José shakes his head ruefully at my purchases.

"Anything you want?" I ask him. I nod at the end-cap displays. "Doritos—four for a dollar! Come on, it's on me."

He laughs. "I'm not hungry."

This is not true. I tear open the fizzy cola bottles and he palms half the bag, swiftly, before I can even protest. "This way," he says, leading me past an electronics store, a dizzying flash of lights and blipping sci-fi-style noises.

"Where?"

"We're supposed to pick up Lucy. Her shift is over in twenty minutes."

I forgot that Lucy works at the mall. I wonder if I have, like, brain damage or something.

She's a "sales associate," as they seem to be called, at one of the Wet Seal outposts. I see her immediately as we approach the store: she's standing at the front wearing a floral skirt, tank top, and the platform flip-flops that are all the rage here. She's talking to a customer, holding out a pair of embellished jeans, pointing out the detailing at the pockets. The customer is smiling.

Lucy is smiling.

She speaks rapid-fire Spanish, offers to start a fitting room for the girl. As she leads the customer to the back of the store, she grabs at a halter top that she explains will be *perfecto* with the jeans.

She seems comfortable, confident, competent. In control, like the Lucy from home, but softer, cheerier. She comes back from the dressing room and spots us standing in the entrance of the store. Her face falls, if only a minuscule amount. There are a million hidden messages in that expression, one of which is that she was expecting José, but me? Not so much. And that while she may not wish me bodily harm, she's not exactly ecstatic to see me. I can read all of this in her face in a split second. But I don't mind because I've got her number.

Sometimes? When she thinks no one is watching? Lucy smiles.

* * *

Marisa is waiting for us on her front steps when we get home. She gives Lucy the full-body press, which Lucy returns. "Good day?" she asks.

"Good day," Lucy says.

I nod. It wasn't bad.

* * *

On Tuesday my mother and I go to San Lorenzo. I've never heard of San Lorenzo, in fact have a hell of a time finding it on any Puerto Rican map, but as it turns out, it's the name of the town where my grandmother grew up. Or rather, the village. *Village* is definitely the more apt term.

The surrounding environs of San Lorenzo are known for producing tobacco and sugarcane, or so I read in *Fodor's*. San Lorenzo itself, near as I can tell, is known for scraggly-looking hills and semi-abandoned housing in various states of disrepair. Not to diss this place or anything, but it's hard to imagine San Lorenzo as a major source of export income. And if this is what it's like now, I can only imagine the thriving metropolis it must have been while my grandmother was growing up.

God, and I spend all my time bitching about the suburban dysfunctions of Westchester. At least I have a car.

My mother—ever more fearless behind the wheel—navigates the winding roads leading up to the patchy hilltops. We're about an hour plus outside of San Juan and we haven't passed another car for miles. What I wouldn't give for a traditionally Puerto Rican misleading and indecipherable road sign. This is the countryside of B-level horror movies. I can see it now: we pop an unexpected flat, pull to the side of the road . . . the next thing you know some three-fingered circus freak is strangling us and abandoning us in a ditch. And shrieking at me in Spanish, of course.

It is possible I'm overreacting. Really this is just a ride in the countryside. The spooky, sparse, and totally unpopulated countryside, sure, but three-fingered circus freaks are in short order here.

At least, I haven't seen any of them. Yet.

"We're here." My mother pulls her car into a makeshift parking spot, interrupting my reverie before I have a chance to take it to new levels of hysteria. She kills the ignition, steps out of the car, sighs. "*This* is where my mother grew up."

I take in the landscape, which as I've mentioned is fairly ratty. The hills are covered with pebbly layers of dirt, and the foliage that adorns the non-grassy, non-knolls hangs lifelessly. It's like a neglected impressionist painting left to wither and die.

"Are you sure she grew up *here?*" I ask. I mean, it seems to me that we're taking a fair amount on faith. After all, it's not like we have a GPS system for confirmation.

My mother shoots me a look that basically means I should quit while I'm ahead. She has some insider's knowledge on the matter. "This is where Rosa told me to look. This is where they would come every year on my mother's birthday." I can tell by her delivery that she's wistful, nostalgic; her mother's birthday ritual was just one more tradition that my mother missed out on when she came to the United States, met my father, decided to forsake her heritage.

Or whatever. I'm still a little bit unclear on the details.

I wonder when my grandmother's birthday was. If it was the summer, I can envision Dora, Ana, Pilar, and Lucy, hair piled high on top of their heads, sweat coating their upper lips, Lucy scowling and shifting her weight from one hip to the other as her grandmother soaked in the history. The view shifts in my mind to a winter tableau—same old same old, but with different weather. In my imagination

Lucy's bundled in a coat that she resents even having to own, coming as she does from San Juan, where the temperature never drops below sixty-five degrees. Dora is wondering whether or not it's going to snow. (Hint: it's Puerto Rico; it's not.) It's maybe sixty degrees, a winter wonderland. They should seal that in a snow globe for me to take back to New York.

"It's a funny story, actually," my mother says, breaking into my thoughts. "She was very young when she arrived here from Spain. She was separated from her parents and raised with extended family somewhere"—she gestures toward the hilltops—"up there. But no one ever knew exactly what day her birthday was. So she celebrated it every Easter."

I raise my eyebrows. I don't know much about the Easter story per se, but it does feel weird to me that someone as devout as my grandmother would have the chutzpah to adopt the Resurrection as her own personal birthright.

"Because it's springtime. And so fresh start-y," my mother clarifies, reading my thoughts and totally freaking me out. "Really, it's a nice sentiment." She delivers this information with confidence.

Okay, so maybe it is a nice sentiment. For a brief and fleeting moment I am sad that I never knew my grandmother at all, much less became acquainted with this semi-whimsical side of her, an aspect of her persona that was forced to speculate on her own personal history. But she had an idea of where she'd come from that for all I knew was more satisfying than the truth.

Pretty impressive.

It occurs to me: for better or for worse, my mother reinvented herself too. Was it, like her mother, out of necessity, personal preference? Or some strange amalgamation of both?

I glance at my mother and am startled to find tears running down her face. She cries silently, but steadily.

I'm not sure what to do. I've never seen her cry before, save for her mother's actual funeral. I was helpless then.

But now?

I don't know. I *really* don't know.

Her sobs are noiseless but full-bodied. Her shoulders tremble softly and her head shakes.

I have to do something.

I am not the "do something" type.

But I have to.

After an uncomfortable beat I reach out and take her hand. She lets me.

It's the only action I can think to take, but it seems to be right.

We slowly make our way over the hills, meandering

without any real overriding purpose. Or at least, no purpose that can take any shape at this moment. The landscape is unvaried. There isn't that much to see. Except, there sort of is. We press on in silence, lost in our respective thoughts.

* * *

"Ready?" my mother asks after a half hour or so. She's mostly gotten her composure back. But I can still see the tracks her tears have cut through her makeup, and the skin underneath her eyes is red and puffy.

"Huh?" I'm completely distracted.

"Are you ready to go?"

I am ready to go. Of course. San Lorenzo has served its purpose. But all at once, I know what I'm going to tell my father.

Today may be one of the only times I've seen my mother cry. But it's also the first time I've ever been able to comfort her.

I'm not ready to leave Puerto Rico. Not right now.

No one could be more surprised than I am myself.

* * *

On the drive home I have an idea. "Let's make dinner," I offer.

My mother glances at me quickly, not wanting to take her eyes off the road. "Rosa said she would take care of it."

"We'll beat them home. It will be a nice surprise." It's

as much of a surprise to me as it would be to anyone. "We can make, um . . ." I pause, search my brain for the right word. After a moment, miraculously, it comes to me. *"Arroz con gandules."*

My mother raises her eyebrows. "You liked it?" She smiles, no doubt recalling the sight of me all but licking my plate clean the other night at Eva's.

"I liked it," I confirm.

My mom reaches over, squeezes my shoulder softly. "I think it's a great idea. Rosa will be impressed," she says.

"Except—I have one condition," I clarify. "We have to add a New York twist."

My mom laughs. "What's that?"

I shrug. "They're always calling me the *nuyorican.* I thought I'd spice things up a bit by making a *nuyorican* meal. Maybe *arroz con gandules*—with dirty water dogs on the side?"

She shakes her head. "We'll be stuffed."

"Nothing wrong with that."

We'll be stuffed, but we'll be happy. It's a great idea.

* * *

Dinner is as successful as I expect; Rosa was taken aback to find our "surprise," but in a good way. I think she and Lucy are going to have to reconsider their idea of me as, well, less than useful. My mother, for her part, seems proud that we showed some initiative, that we contributed something completely on our own.

I can't say what compelled me to tackle *arroz con gandules* (*con* hot dogs). To say that it had anything to do with my mother's little breakdown might be an exaggeration.

But I can't come up with a better explanation.

* * *

I call my father later that night; he's a little bit taken aback but sympathetic, understanding, and ultimately not too sorry to be spared the expense of the plane ticket. Max is more blasé, obviously. "As long as your present is on its way." I promise him that it is and sign off quickly before I can give in to crushing second thoughts. I think to call Noah, to tell him that I'm not coming home after all, and then I remember: I never told him that I was in the first place.

"*Mira,* you got a postcard." Rosa brushes past me and drops a small, colorful rectangle onto the little mail table in the front hallway.

A postcard? I can't remember the last time I got any piece of snail mail. I grab at it eagerly. The image is one of three women in period garb churning butter while soldier types in uniforms stomp past. GREETINGS FROM COLONIAL WILLIAMSBURG. I smile, wondering just what exactly Ade had to promise Izzy to get her way with this little pit stop.

Isabelle is not the type who likes to watch people make jam, quilts, etc. Though she is a sucker for hand-spun cashmere.

I flip the card over. *Don't be fooled—the colonials all wear digital watches and Nikes under their dresses. Must've been one advanced settlement, right? We miss you. Xs.*

I'm overcome with a wave of homesickness, which is silly, because Ade and Izzy aren't even at home. I wouldn't have seen them even if I had taken my father up on his offer. I push away the friend-sick feelings and vow to be merely pleased to have gotten some mail. Take that, Yahoo, and your zero messages. Who's a total loser now?

"Is it from your *boyfriend?*" Ana singsongs.

I shake my head.

"Are you in a fight like Lucy and Rafael?"

Ana's words stop me cold. I'd forgotten that things were allegedly on the rocks with them. Lucy's three younger sisters aren't exactly the most reliable sources, but still . . .

Lucy sits in the living room with a paperback in hand. It's cracked open and she marks the place with her finger, but she's not even looking in the general direction of the book. Instead she stares off into space, impassively. I don't know about Ana's sixth sense—I mean, I probably

wouldn't put money on it—but something's up. No
doubt about it.

I contemplate going over to Lucy and saying something.
What, I have no idea—the last thing she'd want would be
sympathy from the gringa. But it's not like I don't have
some sense of how she must be feeling.

Boys. Do relationships always suck?

Things were never sucky with Noah exactly, but they
were sort of . . . bland. It'd be nice to have real feelings,
strong feelings for someone—as a person more than just a
romantic entity.

I'll bet that Lucy has real feelings for Rafael . . . which
in turn leads to the suckiness.

So unfair, life.

Inexplicably, at the notion of "real feelings," Ricky's face
pops into my head. It's gone almost as quickly as it
appeared, leaving me dazed.

Huh? He makes me laugh, true, but no matter what,
I'm still technically with Noah. At least until we actually
get in touch with each other and decide that we aren't.
Ricky has nothing to do with that, and anyway, this is
about Lucy.

Lucy and *her* romance woes. Not mine.

Lucy snaps out of her trance. She shakes her head,
dog-ears the page in her book, and closes it. She places it

on the coffee table and looks up, in the process making inadvertent eye contact with me. I look down. When I look up again, she shoots me a dirty look, rises, and stalks off to her bedroom.

I decide against approaching her about Rafael, for obvious reasons. Better safe than sorry.

Ten

On Wednesday my mother and I go to the art museum in Old San Juan. Much of what there is to see in Puerto Rico, culturally speaking, at least, is in Old San Juan. Coming from New York, this place is a little smaller scale than what I'm used to, but I have to admit, it's a nice way to spend an afternoon. The bright, bold paintings, most of which are by native artists, are appealing.

I think of Ade and Isabelle at the Washington Mall and how humid it must be. If nothing else, I definitely have the best summer weather here. I bet my hair kicks their hair's ass. I mean, if hair had an ass or whatever.

It's cold comfort, but less so than I would have thought a few weeks ago.

Mom is different too. I can't pinpoint the exact moment

that it happened, but whatever she was looking for out here, she seems to have found it. Maybe it had to do with reconnecting. She felt guilty about leaving her family behind when she went off to college. That would make sense. Now she's made those connections whole again.

* * *

We're home in time for dinner, natch, but Lucy has a surprise for me. "Ricky's coming over tonight," she says.

I flush. I haven't spoken to or about him since my spontaneous spazzy thought of him last night, which of course Lucy would have no way of knowing. I feel self-conscious even still.

"He wants to go see—" She names a summer blockbuster action movie that opened the weekend we left, starring a hipster-come-lately dressed in tights and a cape. A superhero thing.

It's a few weeks old back in New York; I'm sure Noah has already seen it. We would have seen it together if I were, um, there instead of here.

"They have cheap tickets on weeknights at the place down the street," Lucy explains.

"Who's going?" I ask, as though I'm seriously curious about the guest list. Which I sort of am. But only for one reason.

"Pia, Teresa, Ricky, me. You," Lucy says pointedly.

"Ramona has to watch her baby brother."

She doesn't offer up any suggestions as to where Rafael might be or what he might be doing other than seeing the movie with us. I don't ask.

Since that slight glimmer of warmth that I saw back at the mall the other day is all but gone, I choose to give Lucy space, both literal and emotional. I like my head where it is, attached to my neck.

* * *

The movie theater is dingy and much, much dirtier than the antiseptic mall-type multiplexes that have threatened to overtake the Westchester County landscape. But the tickets are five-fifty. Five-fifty! In Westchester the weeknight matinees are seven dollars. It's too bad they are so far behind with their movie releases in San Juan or I'd spend every night here, even with all the gum underneath the seats.

As we take our places, Ricky asks if I want anything to eat. I'm not hungry at all, but I have an almost Pavlovian response to entering a movie theater: I'm instantaneously overwhelmed by a craving for popcorn.

I nod, dig into my bag for some cash. He pushes me off. "I've got it."

I'd rather he not—it's too date-like—but he's gone before I can protest further. He asks everyone else what they want, which at least makes him seem less like my own personal cabana boy, but they demur. Lucy rolls her eyes. I have utterly failed in winning her over.

"I hope the line's not too long," I say, trying desperately to fill the awkward silence. "I don't want him to miss the coming attractions."

Teresa laughs, flips her long blond hair over one shoulder. "Don't worry, movies here start on Puerto Rico time. Like everything else."

She means late; this much I know.

"Even the commercials won't start for at least another"—she frowns at her watch—"twenty minutes."

She's right: fifteen minutes later Ricky's back with popcorn and a Coke the size of a swimming pool. I'm slightly disappointed that it's regular, not diet, but I don't exactly feel right saying so. "I love this actor," Ricky tells me, which surprises me somehow. I didn't figure him for the last-action-hero type. I'm a little surprised to find that I even considered his "type" at all.

"He's Noah's favorite too," I say reflexively, because he is. But why bring up Noah now? The name floats out of my mouth, into the air, and drops like an anvil with a thud. At least, in my head it does.

"Noah?"

"The boyfriend," I clarify.

"Ah," Ricky says. If he's in any way bothered by the

mention, he's covering really well. I myself am completely confused. What sort of weird, reverse speech impediment caused me to bring up Noah? No clue. Perhaps it's worth thinking about, but just then the theater goes black and a trio of boldly dressed Latina women fill the screen, trilling about their favorite soft drink. The movie has started, or at least the commercials have. I need to pay attention. Put all thoughts of Noah—and Ricky—out of my mind.

Focus, I tell myself sternly. Hot guys in tights, after all. That should help get my mind off anything. I cross my fingers and stick them into the pockets of my hoodie, where no one else can see this furtive bit of superstition.

* * *

Ricky is one of our two drivers, Lucy the second. Through some bizarre confluence of the cosmos, Ricky decides to ignore the fact that driver the second is actually my host for the summer and would therefore make the more-logical choice of chauffeur. He offers me shotgun. Lucy makes a pissy face—and says that Teresa needs to get home early. She's obviously suggesting that Ricky make it his priority to get Teresa home posthaste.

"If that's the case," Ricky says, undeterred, "then you should take her. I want pizza."

"Ooh," I say impulsively. Pizza sounds *fantastic*. I don't care what the Puerto Rican interpretation of the classic

Italian fast food is; I just know that I want some, and I want it now.

I also don't care that Lucy is shooting daggers at me. Well, I don't care much, anyway. It's been a while since I've gone for a late-night munchie run. It's a very suburban thing to do. Ade and I would split cheese fries. I wonder, do they have cheese fries in Puerto Rico? If so, would Ricky share them with me?

"You're hungry?" Ricky laughs. I nod. I feel like a cartoon character whose thought bubble is visible to the entire viewing audience. I'm seeing Lucy trussed up as a turkey or decorated in slices of pepperoni. I wasn't hungry before the movie, that's true, but sharing popcorn with Ricky seems to have awoken some sort of latent appetite.

Ricky laughs, as he always does when he's sort of seeing through my thoughts.

Again, I'm surprised to have an "always" thought about Ricky.

"Then it's settled." He turns to Lucy. "You can take Pia and Teresa home. Emily and I will get pizza."

"But—"

"Do you want pizza too?" Ricky asks. It's a smart tactic: she can't brat about it if he includes her. Then again, knowing Ricky, it probably isn't a tactic as much as just him being an all-around thoughtful guy.

Lucy opens her mouth to reply—something tells me she'd rather gouge herself in the eye with a knitting needle than send me out for pizza with Ricky alone—but before she can answer, Teresa jumps in. "No way, Luce. My mom's going to kill me if I'm any later, and you promised if I came out, you would get me home in time."

Lucy seethes. Her eyes narrow into tiny slits, but she acquiesces. A few moments more and I'm strapped into the shotgun seat of Ricky's car after all. Lucy and her friends pile into Lucy's car. I wonder briefly what I've gotten myself into, and I have a feeling, as Lucy's car pulls smoothly out of its parking spot, that she's wondering the exact same thing.

* * *

Pizza in Puerto Rico isn't all that different from pizza on the mainland. At least, not if you go to Pizza Hut. It's nice to know that franchises are the same all over. Nice in sort of a scary way, that is. In the event of a nuclear holocaust the only things left standing will be cockroaches, Starbucks, and chain restaurants. It is a comforting thought.

Ricky and I share a pie, half veggie, half pepperoni. I'm not a vegetarian and I'm certainly not kosher, but the fluorescent orange hue of the pepperoni makes me shudder. I try not to gag as he shovels the entire half pie down his throat at warp speed.

"You must have a crazy metabolism," I say.

He grins and wipes a smudge of grease off his chin. "What? I'm a growing boy." In that case, I think, he has a lot more growing to do—he's just barely bigger than I am—but it's endearing, definitely.

"Noah would never . . ." I trail off. *What* is wrong with me? Why do I constantly need to bring up Noah? Do I have some sort of mental disorder, like those people who are in car accidents who forget how to say everything except for one word? Super.

My entire thought, FYI, is, *Noah would never eat half a pizza without worrying about the fat and calories.* Does that make me like Noah more or less? Interesting question.

"Is he a wrestler or something? I thought those were the only guys who watch their weight," Ricky says.

"No," I tell him. "He's not. I guess he's just . . . vain?"

As I say it, I realize it's true. And also that it bothers me a little bit. I try to laugh it off. Ricky is kind enough not to press.

"How did you guys leave things for the summer?" he asks. So much for not pressing.

I toy with my fork, dragging grease trails across my plate. "We didn't."

Except for our extended game of phone tag, that is.

"I mean, I guess we didn't come to any decisions. Why

would we? We didn't know I would be away all summer. So I guess . . . that means . . . things are still . . . on," I say with a complete and total lack of confidence.

"But?" he leads.

"But it's weird," I admit. "We haven't really been able to talk—it's been total phone tag—and the thing is that next year, I'm going away to college and so is he."

"To a different school."

"Yeah. I'll be at Brown, in Rhode Island. He's going to Northeastern, in Boston."

"Not too far apart," he says. At my look he says, "What? I'm not allowed to know some things?"

"What about you?" I ask, tired of being in the hot seat.

"What *about* me?" he asks, adopting an innocent posture.

"What about you and Lucy? You two never got together?" They have such a familiarity with each other that it's hard to believe they never did. Also, it would explain her annoying possessiveness.

Ricky shrugs. "We did." He looks sheepish. "But that was back in elementary school."

"Oh, you were like her fifth-grade boyfriend?" I tease.

He blushes. "Something like that." He sighs. "Rafael came to our school in sixth grade, and that was it."

I whistle. "Really? They've been together that long?"

"Oh, yeah. They're the real deal. They get each other."

I can see what he means, even from the little time I've spent with the two of them. What's more is that he doesn't sound at all wistful or jealous, just matter-of-fact. Which is cool. I've never had much luck with platonic guy friends myself. Which begs the question of what Ricky is becoming to me.

"What are your friends doing this summer?" he asks, and for some reason, I'm surprised that it even occurs to him to ask. It's a nice reminder that I do have friends, a place where I belong. That I seem like the type of person who would have those things.

"Road trip," I say, struggling to keep my voice neutral. "They're probably"—I check my watch as though their itinerary is printed on its face—"halfway to Chicago right now."

"You were supposed to go with them?" It's a question, but one that he knows the answer to.

I nod. "Yeah. But then . . ." I trail off. Then my grandmother died. A fact that still hasn't hit me with the appropriate gravitas. At the time it was unfathomable that I would reschedule my summer for a woman I'd never met, a woman I'd been led to believe didn't mean all that much to my mother. A woman who, I had deduced, my mother left behind to pursue a different lifestyle. But now . . . now it's hard to picture myself in the backseat of the car with the girls. The image in my mind is growing blurrier with every day that passes. True, Lucy hasn't exactly welcomed me into the fold, but I feel, in some odd way, *right,* right where I am.

"But then I came here," I finish lamely. I pick up the leftover crust of my pizza, contemplate taking a bite, and decide better of it. I put it back down on my plate, push the plate aside.

"Well, the great outdoors will always be there," Ricky says, wisely leaving off the part where my friends and their itinerary may not be.

I'm suddenly homesick and overly full. I shake my head, take one last sip of diet soda. Yak. Diet Coke tastes like chemical sludge. I don't know why I drink it. I guess it's just something that girls do.

Ricky senses my abrupt change in mood. "Ready to go?" he asks graciously, as though it had been his idea all along. I am overwhelmed by his perceptiveness, adore him just a little for it.

* * *

We toss our trash, step outside. The air in the parking lot is crisp, cleaner than the dingy environs would suggest. His car, a "spunky" two-door Ford Escort that has definitely seen better days, is on the far side of the lot. We cross the blacktop briskly, my flip-flops making a smacking sound that punctuates my every step. I can't think of anything to say that wouldn't be stupid. The moment feels pregnant, tense, brimming with potential and unspoken promises. I can't put my finger on why.

Ricky comes around to my side of the car, leans past my body to open the door for me. It's an old-school gesture, charming. Noah's car has automatic locks, which I guess shouldn't preclude chivalry but somehow does.

Ricky turns the key in the lock, pulls at the handle, opens the door just enough so it sits just slightly ajar, waiting for me to get in. Then he steps back.

All at once Ricky is standing upright and I realize that he is very close to me. So close that I can smell him, mostly shampoo, a green, earthy smell that is distinctly masculine, mingling with a sharply sweet, antiseptic odor. Aftershave? His breath reverberates off my cheek softly. He is looking at me, a sidelong glance out of his peripheral vision. It's a look that I recognize but vaguely, like I'm seeing it through a soft-focus lens.

Quickly, almost instantly, Ricky's face has dipped in toward mine. In a flash it registers—he is trying to kiss me!

I'm stunned, but not surprised. Confused, but eager. Hesitant, but racked with guilt. I have no idea what to do.

I dodge just in time, shrinking backward. It's awkward.

Ricky has to stop himself from tilting too far forward. He pauses mid-swoop, straightens again, coughs for good measure. He looks over my head, behind me, off to one side. Anywhere but my eyes. Which is a relief and also torture.

"Sorry," I say. It sounds tinny and pathetic, suspended between us in the thick air. What was refreshing a moment ago has become cloying, suffocating. What am I sorry for? Any number of things. But the apology can really only do so much. It doesn't dispel the awkwardness.

Mercifully Ricky says nothing, only circles the car back to the driver's side. He gets in, buckles up his seat belt, and I do the same.

* * *

The ride home is one of the longest of my life. For once I wish Ricky were more of a traditional Puerto Rican driver—faster, more aggressive. He pumps the brakes for every yield, cranes his head methodically at every turn. I fidget, twisting the rings on my fingers, fiddling with the zipper on my bag.

I am desperate for someone to say something, for something to happen. But all that happens is that Ricky decides to try the radio. Something, anything, to kill this hideous silence. My bright pink elephant is here with us right now, balanced precariously on the hand rest, trumpeting loudly between us. The radio explodes into a burst of static quickly replaced by a blaring remixed beat. Ricky coughs again, turns it off. I want to laugh and choke back the impulse wisely, but not without effort.

He signals; we turn onto my street. Well, of course it's not my own, but somehow I've come to think of it that way. He pulls into my (there's that word again) driveway and puts the car in park. He leaves the engine running.

"Um, thanks," I say, my voice hoarse. "It was great having pizza."

Egad. *It was great having pizza?* You'd think I'd been raised by a nomadic tribe of tree dwellers. I cringe.

"Yeah," Ricky says, short, noncommittal. He doesn't sound angry as such. Just deeply detached. It's unsettling. "Glad you liked it."

I grab my door handle, click open the door. The rush of night air is a stark contrast to the climate-controlled environment of the car, but it's welcome nonetheless. I think I'm choking. Siddhartha probably never had AC, I think wildly. Siddhartha. Almost forgot about him.

This is the mental equivalent of babbling, this train of nonsensical thought. I gather myself, take a deep breath. I peek at Ricky through the corner of my eye. His gaze is focused; he stares directly forward, as though willing himself not to falter, not to cave and look my way. I realize: this moment is overwhelming and not in a good way, but there's nothing to be done about it now. "See you soon," I say, too softly for him to hear me clearly.

I step out of the car, and it's all I can do not to dart up the front steps. I pace myself, force myself very deliberately to walk like a normal person or as normal as I can be now that I've been possessed by the spirit of someone much, much spazzier than I. When I get to the front door, I grab at it, open it, step eagerly into the foyer. I fight the urge to glance back over my shoulder. Only after I'm inside do I collapse back against the door.

* * *

I'm listlessly nursing a cup of lukewarm coffee the next morning when my mother comes into the kitchen. "Good morning, sleepyhead," she says, smiling. My mother has never been one to smile in the morning, not even under the best of circumstances. This is an interesting development. I must say that the island agrees with her.

"Morning," I mutter. I'm too preoccupied with running through the events of last night to make idle conversation.

"You got in late last night," she comments.

"I didn't realize I woke you. Sorry."

"You didn't. Well, just for a minute. But it was no problem. Did you like the movie?"

Suddenly I go blank, can't even recall what movie we watched. Oh, right.

"Uh, yeah," I tell her. "It was . . . action-y."

"What are the movie theaters like here?"

"Same as movie theaters back home," I snap, surprising myself. What is up my butt? I am not one to talk to my mother that way.

Fortunately, she chooses to ignore my minor temper tantrum. "I'm going to shower," she says. "Rosa took the girls this morning."

"Cool," I say, feeling guilty but unsure of how to go about apologizing. Sometimes I am such an ass. Not often, but sometimes. More and more lately, I guess.

My mother exits the room without fanfare just as Lucy is entering. "Don't you have work?" I ask.

"I'm doing a later shift today," she says. "*¿Qué pasa?* What did you say to your mother?"

"Huh?"

Lucy shrugs. "She looked upset."

Okay, so I wasn't super-polite and perky at this semi-ungodly hour, first thing in the morning. But please. It's not like I freaked out on my mother or anything. Lucy is totally overreacting. For a change.

Of course, so am I. I'm totally having an internal tirade. More mental babbling. *Perfecto.*

"It's nothing," I brat. Not that it's any of Lucy's business.

"Sure, whatever," she says.

"What does that mean?" I ask, trying but failing somewhat to keep the edge from creeping into my voice. I'm overtired and apparently more than a little crabby and confused about the events of the previous night.

"Nothing," Lucy says. She adds under her breath but loud enough for me to hear, "Just that I wouldn't expect you to care about someone else's feelings."

My skin prickles; my blood boils, tingling in my veins. I hate, hate, hate conflict, would rather douse myself in hot oil than deal, but Lucy is pushing exactly the wrong buttons. She's jealous, I know, of the fact that Ricky likes me. She's pissed that I blew him off—though how she *knows* I blew him off, I have no idea. Either she's making an incredibly lucky guess or they talked this morning. Either way, screw it. Screw her. Does she think this is easy for me? Any of this? That I wanted to hurt Ricky in any way?

I haven't been this furious in a good, long time.

"What would you know about it?" I say. My voice is low, but my tone is unmistakable. "You're so *totally* open-minded." Not exactly fighting words, I know, but for me, it's practically a physical assault. I'm shaking with nerves, rage, frustration.

"You're such a princess," Lucy hisses. "Everything is easy for you."

"Right," I say. I rise, somehow manage to deposit my coffee mug into the sink without shattering it into a thousand tiny porcelain shards the way that the fantasy me is dying to do, and storm out of the room. "You're exactly right."

That second part I say in my head, naturally.

Eleven

My mother is still in the shower; I can hear the rush of water coming from the direction of the bathroom. Lucy has disappeared into her bedroom, and I have nothing to say to her right now anyway. Or at least nothing pleasant. In my head I've begun and abandoned several scathing diatribes that I know I'll never have the guts to speak out loud.

We decide to visit El Yunque for the afternoon, the rain forest. We drive the two hours, watching through the windshield as the landscape evolves from desolate strip malls to rickety low-income housing and finally to twisting, winding roads leading into lush, leafy mountains. The car winds up a hill, slow and steep.

We watch a little filmstrip in the visitor center. ("The

coquí is a small amphibian that inhabits El Yunque; you can hear its cry if you listen closely.") Then we decide to hike.

I must confess, I am not much for the physical activity. Back home I am occasionally talked into a half hour on the elliptical machine when Isabelle is facing an "obesity crisis." But left to my own devices, I'm very sedentary. I huff as we make our way up the craggy inclines of the hiking path.

"Are you sure this is the easy trail?" I gasp, weary.

"Emily!" my mother exclaims. "It's only been twenty minutes. Besides, I'm the smoker."

"Not today," I point out.

"And I think, soon, not anymore." She smiles. "It's nice, isn't it?"

I stumble, regain my footing. She reaches out, touches my elbow as if to steady me. It's a beat too late, but it feels good anyway.

"It is nice," I agree.

She points over the railing, over a ravine. All manner of trees poke, prod, and lean, as if the rain forest could come alive at any moment. She taps the edge of a bumpy, squashed-looking plant. "It's breadfruit," she says.

"Someone was paying attention to the filmstrip."

"You *do* realize that this is my home, don't you?" my mother asks.

I do. I stare at her for a moment. I do, and I don't.

"We should have brought our bathing suits," she muses. "We could have gone in. There's a waterfall at the topmost peak of the rain forest."

I've seen pictures. Supposedly it's breathtaking. But I don't know what my mother is thinking; I, for one, am not sorry about "forgetting" our suits. In addition to avoiding strenuous activity, I'm also not one for getting my hair wet when styling products are not close at hand.

* * *

When we come home, I'm in an inexplicably good mood. I decide to try Noah.

I had a good day. It'd be nice to tell him about it, I think.

Miraculously, he picks up on the second ring.

"Noah!" I forget my promise to myself to play it cool; it's been over three weeks since I've heard his voice live and in concert. I'm delirious, geeky, and heady with excitement. God, I'm such a dork. Yesterday I wasn't even sure if I really liked him.

"Hello?" He sounds confused, sleepy.

"Noah, it's me," I say, determined to miss the confusion in his voice. Noah was never really one for catching the worm, if I recall correctly. But it's 4 p.m. Maybe he was taking a mid-afternoon nap? A late-afternoon nap?

"Babe! How is it down there?" His voice still sounds

fuzzy and thick with sleep, but at least some recognition is in there, I realize, breathing hard.

"Hot," I say, illogically. "It's hot down here. But in a good way. I mean, there's not too much humidity. Good hair and stuff." Dear Lord. What the hell am I talking about? "So," I continue, speaking too quickly, "how are things? What's new up there?"

"Aw, the usual," he says. "You missed a good party last weekend. Shana's house."

Shana Rivers is tall, redheaded, thin. A cheerleader. A party at her house is considered a big-time thing. It's not great news that I missed it, worse news that Noah went without me. Not that I blame him. What was he supposed to do, sit at home and stare at my pictures? *There's* an interesting mental image.

Anyway, he's not the cheating type. I don't think. It dawns on me: neither am I. But just barely, apparently.

I wouldn't have thought that before now. That he would cheat, I mean. Or that I would. I wouldn't have thought anything like that before I up and left for an entire summer, without any level of clarity whatsoever.

But I have no one but myself to blame. And besides, I'm the one who almost sort-of kissed someone else last night.

"I'm glad you had fun," I tell him.

"It would have been more fun if you'd been there."

And there it is. The reassurance I've been looking for. It's not exactly poetry, yet it's real. I heard it. The question is, is it enough?

"I know," I tell him.

Speaking of too little, too late . . .

"Your brother said you were coming home."

"He did?" I yelp.

Aw, man. Screw Max. I mean, unless he was really speaking out of wishful thinking, in which case, I guess that's cute and sweet and sort of sad.

"Um, well, it was a thought. But . . . "

"You were going to come home for his birthday."

"It was just an idea that my dad had," I hedge. "But it didn't make a whole lot of sense. I mean"—I'm grasping—"to fly home on Wednesday for his birthday on Thursday, then to come back Saturday for the rest of the summer?"

"Yeah?"

He's not making this any easier. I think he's offended by the idea that it wasn't worth coming home to see him. I get it; I'd be offended if the tables were turned.

"Well, that's a lot of money for a quick little getaway, don't you think?"

"Since when do you care about your parents' money?" he asks. As though I'm some sort of over-privileged refugee

from *The OC.* Come to think of it, I really should intro-
duce Noah to Lucy. The two of them could have a long
conversation about my perceived shortcomings. And what
with the way she's been fighting with Rafael . . .

"Well, it's not just that," I backpedal, for some reason
incapable of even disagreeing with Noah when I'm sure he's
being unreasonable. "My mom really needs me."

This is categorically Not True. If my mother needed me
down here a few weeks ago, these days she's much stronger.
She's gone from a pack a day to two cigarettes a day, and if I
had to guess, I'd say she's about a week away from being
down to one a day. It's reassuring. Whatever it was that she
was looking for down here, it looks like she is finding it.
She's the one who wanted to plunge headfirst into the
waterfall, after all.

Meanwhile, my relationship with my boyfriend is disin-
tegrating before my very eyes (or, at least, before my very
cellular connection), and I've pissed off one of the few people down here who seems to genuinely like me. And—oh,
yeah—I've pissed off Lucy too. Not that it was such a difficult task, but still.

"Huh," Noah grunts noncommittally. It's uninspiring.
And—actually—a little bit annoying.

I try to change the subject. "My cousin Lucy has been
really weird. Well, weirder than usual, anyway, these past

few days. I guess mostly she was hostile before. The weird-
ness is something altogether new."

"I thought she was the unfriendly one anyway," Noah
fills in.

"Oh. I told you about that?" I ask. Have I talked to
Noah since I've been in Puerto Rico? I don't remember it.
Have I had some kind of mini-stroke?

"No, Ade mentioned it," Noah says. "She said that you
told her."

Right, Ade. Right.

"Have you spoken to them?" I ask. He knows exactly
who "they" are, in this context.

"Not lately. I've been, you know, mostly busy with stuff
around here."

"Well, out of sight, out of mind, I guess. Shana Rivers's
parties and whatever," I say—or try to say—lightly. I'm kidding, but it's an opening for Noah. An opening that he does
not take.

"Yeah." He laughs, a heartier laugh than I'm comfortable with. After a beat it dies down; he coughs, sniffs, clears
his throat. "Anyway, what time is it down there?"

I'm illogically irked. "Um, there's, you know, no time
difference." Four p.m. is a perfectly acceptable time to call
one's maybe, sort-of-still boyfriend, isn't it? And why is he
so concerned with the time? He hasn't spoken to me in

weeks. If he isn't going to display exuberance, at least he could try to avoid outright *impatience.* Maybe Shana Rivers is waiting for him, I think. It's not a fair thought, but it's in and out of my head before I even have a chance to really process it.

"Right. Well, I've got . . . soccer . . . in an hour, so I'd better go take a shower."

Take a shower *before* soccer? Right.

"Cool, have fun," I chirp, forcing myself to stay upbeat. *I am not irked by my boyfriend. I am not irked by my boyfriend. I am not irked by my boyfriend.*

That is, if he even is still my boyfriend. Or if I still want him to be.

"Well, I should be home in a couple of weeks," I finish, still with the desperate, slightly crazed attempt to sound breezy. "See you then?" Do I even want to see him then? All things considered?

"Definitely, babe," he says, and hangs up the phone. And just like that, our conversation is over.

* * *

Either my mother is *still* in the shower, or she's come out and is now off doing something else entirely. Our room is empty when I come back to it, though I notice that the bed has been made up nicer than in a hotel. Hospital corners and everything. Mom does love to be tidy. I wish more of that would rub off on me. Fitted sheets are my enemy.

I step outside for some fresh air. There's nothing going on out here either, just Pilar and Marisa playing house. They've done up an old tree stump to look like a dinner table. Obviously Pilar is practicing to take over for me when my mother and I go back to New York.

Marisa is humming under her breath but stops when she sees me. "You look sad," she says, and not for the first time, I curse her perceptiveness. The mouths of babes, yadda yadda . . .

"I had a fight with my boyfriend," I say. "Sort of."

Her forehead scrunches up in surprise. "You have a boyfriend?"

"Yeah," I say, not sure why this is cause for such utter confusion and disbelief. "Sort of."

"Oh," she says, as if she actually couldn't care less. "It's just I thought you liked Ricky."

Oh. Right. That.

* * *

I flip my phone shut, toss it into my regular daytime tote bag. I contemplate clearing the call log so as to remove the temptation to obsess over my failed communication with Noah, but it's not worth the effort. Besides, I'll probably obsess either way.

I wonder what's on the schedule for this evening. I'm

sure nothing groundbreaking, more of the same, but inexplicably, I'm in the mood for some sightseeing. I think there's a fort somewhere in Old San Juan that we still haven't visited. It's a gorgeous night, *por supuesto*. Warm and breezy. Could be just the thing. I have a hankering to buy cheap beaded earrings from a local girl selling from a cart on the side of the road, and Old San Juan has no shortage of those: earrings, carts, girls, forts. You name it, I'm game. Which is a fairly new—and welcome—sensation.

I head to the bathroom feeling oddly refreshed, hearing the shower run, turn the doorknob. My mother won't mind me talking to her while she finishes up; it's something we do all the time at home during the whole chaotic morning crush. Come to think of it, it's sort of strange that we never do it here. I guess we really have settled into a new routine. I barge into the bathroom. "Ma, do you think we could—"

I stop abruptly. It's not my mother in the bathroom; it's Lucy. And while the shower is running, she herself is crouched over the toilet, leaning so far into her cell phone that I think she's going to swallow it. The look on her face is thunderous. I have no idea who she's talking to, of course, but she's having trouble getting a word in edgewise. And she is clearly not happy about it.

"*Ay, no, pero—*"

"*Creo que—*"

"No sé for certain, *pero—"*

"¡Mira, creo que estoy embarazada!"

I cough, trip, stumble forward against the door. She looks up, startled. *"Get out of here!"* she hisses, waving her free hand at me impatiently.

Once I've got my footing again, I do. I stagger backward and pull the door shut closed behind me, breathing heavily. I'm stunned. I'm not sure which is the more shocking news: that I understood all of Lucy's one-sided conversation or the content of the conversation itself. It's really a toss-up. And for the umpteenth time since I've arrived in Puerto Rico, I've got a problem that I have literally less than no idea how to deal with. Never mind that the problem is actually Lucy's.

Lucy thinks she may be pregnant.

Twelve

L *ucy is pregnant.*

Or she thinks she is, and she doesn't strike me as the hysterical, drama-queen type. I mean, sure, she loves to go all *Mean Girls* on me, but I don't think . . . Well, I saw the look on her face just now. It was only for an instant, but there was no mistaking her expression. She definitely thinks there is reason to be worried. Which is, if you ask me, almost as bad as whether or not she really *is* pregnant.

I don't know why the thought strikes me as heresy. As much as I know of Tía Rosa, she would strangle Rafael in his sleep if she knew he had defiled her daughter. She's very religious and definitely anti-premarital naughtiness. So I just assumed that Lucy—upstanding, responsible, mature Lucy—had adhered to her widowed mother's wishes.

Then again, this is the same Lucy who sneaks out to salsa clubs on weeknights, I remind myself. It's not beyond the realm of comprehension that she would ever defy her mother. And it sort of makes sense, the whole pregnancy scare thing, in light of how off things have been with her and Rafael. I feel suddenly, unspeakably bad for Lucy, though I know she'd probably resent my sympathy.

I don't even want to think about how Noah would react if I were in the same boat, but thankfully I don't have to. It's one of the upsides of being miles away from one's boyfriend—both physically and emotionally.

I have to forcibly bring myself back, to remind myself that this latest crisis has nothing to do with me; this is Lucy's thing. I'm guessing she was on the phone with Rafael. It could have been a friend, I suppose, but my limited experience with Lucy and her whole gang tells me that he's the only one that gets her as riled up as this. The expression on her face was a Rafael-inspired special.

Though these are extenuating circumstances. Who knows? Maybe all bets are off.

I have to talk to her. I'm not sure how—I'm anti-confrontation under the best of circumstances, and these are hardly the best of circumstances. I have no reason to believe that Lucy, who doesn't even want makeup tips from me, is looking for my help in a situation like this.

I mean, I could always go find my mother, tell her about the Old San Juan plan, go back to my original agenda for the evening.

But . . .

I can't. I know I can't. Even if Lucy doesn't want to hear from me—even if my advice is one step down from no advice at all—I can't pretend I didn't hear her on the phone. For one thing, it'd be an insult to both of our intelligences.

The bathroom door slams and I hear footsteps. Lucy is walking back to her bedroom. Well, not her bedroom exactly, since that's where my mother and I are sleeping—

I cut the mental babbling off at the pass, square my shoulders, inhale deeply. This is my moment.

I follow Lucy down the hall, padding just far enough behind her that she's not aware of being semi-stalked. It's not an especially long walk, which is a shame, because I use these last few moments to pull together my little speech. Now I'm standing in her doorway, throat dry, any semblance of speech all but forgotten.

Lucy roots in her drawer for a clean pair of socks. Fishing one out, she turns, sees me standing in her doorway. She gasps and jumps a few inches. *"Ay,* are you spying on me, *primita?"*

Primita is a term of endearment. It's pretty clear that she's using it sarcastically.

Whatever. I take another deep breath, plunge onward. "It's just"—I shift my weight from one foot to the other— "it's just that I heard you on the phone."

Her eyes narrow. "So you *were* spying on me?"

"Well, no," I say, defensive but tentative. "I mean, it wasn't intentional. But Lucy—I heard your conversation." I gaze at her meaningfully. "I *understood* it."

She shrugs. "Right. I'll bet you did."

I absorb the insult. "I know that you"—I drop my voice—"think that you're—"

"*Mira!*" she says, cutting me off. "It's really none of your business."

"I'm not *trying* to be in your business," I protest. "But that sounds like, um, some pretty heavy stuff. And I just . . . I mean, I know we haven't exactly been close since I've gotten here, but I just want you to know that I'm here for you."

I swallow, the noise reverberating loudly in my ears. The moment is—for lack of a better word—pregnant.

"I'm here," I say. "If, ah, you want me to be."

She sighs, drawing out the breath. She crosses to the doorway where I stand, and for a moment I actually think there's a chance. A chance that I've gotten through to her, a chance that she's going to say something back to me. That we're going to have a Talk about her Problem, and I'm going to be able to Help her. But once she's standing opposite me in the doorway, she reaches out. For a moment I even think she's going to slap me. I flinch, but she just grabs at the door and swings it shut in my face.

"I'm fine," she snaps, just before the latch clicks into place. "Now leave me alone."

* * *

The next day passes in a blur. Lucy goes to work and drives her sisters to camp. Tía Rosa heads off to her job. José does not make an appearance; he must be caught up in the girlfriend or something. I forget to suggest Old San Juan to my mother, and instead we spend our morning at the supermarket, squeezing produce and pawing through cuts of chicken. When we get back to the house, I try to read but find myself skipping over the same sentence time and again. After half an hour on the same page, I give up, head out for the pool. I drag Pilar's rubber raft into the center of the pool and climb on top of it, floating.

I'm useless. My mom's little breakdown in San Lorenzo had nothing to do with me. The best I could do was to hold her hand. And Lucy, well . . . Lucy wouldn't take my hand if her life depended on it. I can't help anyone. Not even when I desperately want to.

I paddle with one hand, making listless circles over and over again.

I can't think of anything better to do.

* * *

Lucy's home for dinner, of course. The meal is a forced affair, even if I'm the only one who notices. I'm acutely aware of every scrape of silverware against china, every swallow, every crunch. It's like watching dinner through a super-focus microscope, like a movie in surround sound.

After dinner is weirder still; we do the dishes. Lucy washes, I dry. The silence is overpowering, suffocating. I have never not looked at someone as intensely as I am not looking at Lucy.

We finish the dishes. I wring out the dish towel and hang it on its little hook over the sink. I am overwhelmed by how badly I want to say something. But I don't. I've exceeded my outreach quota for the week. Perhaps even for the summer. I rub my hands against the front of my pants—the terry ones again—and am puzzled by the noise the rubbing makes. It's thick and wet, the sound of a dog rooting through the trash. That's when I realize that the noise has nothing to do with my pants.

The sound is Lucy, crying.

She cries somewhat noisily, though I'm clearly meant not to notice. She keeps her head bent low over the sink, bites her lip. After a beat or two she rubs her fist into the corners of her eyes, one after the other. She sniffs once more, shakes her head (as if to say, "No, I wasn't crying"), and coughs. She double-checks the faucet to be sure that it's off, wrenches it in place forcefully. Two residual drops snake their way out of the tap and hit the basin with the tiniest of echoes. Satisfied, Lucy retreats to her bedroom without another word.

* * *

Three days pass in excruciating silence. Lucy and I have both been reduced to automatons, wordlessly carrying out our respective household chores. To the casual observer, I'm guessing it would seem like nothing's wrong. To anyone who knows me, only my bitten-down fingernails would give me away; after all, me being quiet is not a huge, cataclysmic, unheard-of event.

And Lucy? Well, I don't know what the norm is for Lucy, but I would guess that it isn't this ephemeral fluctuation between a vacant, glassy-eyed stare and a practiced stoniness that sets my teeth on edge. No one else in the house seems to notice it. Or if they do, they sure don't say anything. So I don't say anything either. Just dry the dishes and bite my lip. Sometimes hard enough to taste blood.

* * *

It's late, after dinner, and Lucy and I have long since finished our wash-dry routine. My mother and Tía Rosa are out, pitching in for the food drive at Rosa's church. My mother is social action chair at our synagogue back home; I wonder if being involved in the church food drive feels odd, or oddly familiar, to her.

I am scribbling a postcard to Max—Puerto Rican beefcakes sprawled on a beach, WISH YOU WERE HERE spelled out in sunblocked letters across their backs— when I spy my mother's Camel Lights tossed casually on the living-room table. All I can think of is how people say that smoking eases tension. And I'd really like to do that right about now.

What the hell? Lucy is reading to her sisters in bed, and Mom and Rosa won't be back for at least another hour. I swipe the pack and head outside.

* * *

Once I'm there, though, I can't bring myself to do it. I fire up the lighter, stare at the flame, entranced, bring it close to the tip of the cigarette. *Click.* The flame disappears, swallowed back up inside the lighter. I tap my fingers impatiently against the box of cigarettes in my lap, jiggle my crossed legs up and down so that the box bounces. *Click.* Now I'm captivated, watching the flame fan bright, then dim. *Click.* Way more interesting than smoking, which always seems about as appealing as licking the bottom of an ashtray. I always wished it didn't look so . . . well, *cool.*

"Can I get a light?"

I leap in my seat, sending the lighter and the cigarettes clattering to the ground, respectively. Lucy chuckles or at least does a damn good impersonation of a chuckle. "Didn't mean to scare you."

"You didn't . . ." I start, but trail off since, I mean, it's pretty obvious that she *did.* I run through my mental database of pre-rehearsed scripts, but every opening line seems insufficient. I swallow, sigh, offer a half-dozen false starts. I finally settle on, "Are you okay?"

She shrugs, looks down. "Not really." I want to shake my head, Q-Tip my ears, so surprised am I to hear her admit this. Then Lucy does something even more amazing. She squares her shoulders, tossing her hair back in the now-familiar gesture of defiance. Defiance or preparation. She looks me dead in the eyes. "It's just . . ." She starts to turn her head again but redirects her gaze so that we're still focused on each other. "It's just, I need your help."

What do I say? What should I say? What *can* I say?

"Of course."

Thirteen

The thing is that when I say I will help Lucy, I mean it. But I am poorly equipped to do so. Really, really poorly. My experience with these sorts of things is based entirely on what I've seen on the WB. None of my friends back home have had to deal with anything remotely like this. Or if they did, they kept it to themselves. Now I find myself wondering. . . .

But that's hardly the point, of course. The point is that Lucy—*Lucy!*—has come to me asking for help. This is momentous. I mean, she must be desperate. And I'm resourceful enough. Together we should be able to figure something out.

I put the cigarette that I've been toying with back in the box, totally intact. Obviously I was never serious about taking up this new little hobby.

"Well, first things first," I say, adopting a falsely chipper tone. "Are you *sure* that you're pregnant?"

Lucy shakes her head. "It's just that I'm always . . . regular."

"Do you have reason to believe that you're pregnant?" I press, like I've suddenly been possessed by the spirit of a school nurse.

She raises an eyebrow. "I'm always *regular*," she repeats stonily, as if she's speaking to the severely brain-damaged.

"Right," I say, choosing to ignore the fact that she is being slightly pissy. I have to cut her some slack. After all, this is a pretty stressful situation and it *is* Lucy. A certain degree of grouchiness is to be expected.

"Well, I guess the first thing to do is to figure out whether or not you really are pregnant."

"I'm not going to a doctor," she says, crossing her arms over her chest. "The doctor would tell my mom, and my mom would kill me."

"They're not allowed to do that," I say. "Confidentiality and whatever."

Lucy's response is yet another raised eyebrow.

"But I don't think that's necessary anyway," I say hurriedly. "We can just get you a pregnancy test."

Lucy's eyes widen as though I've suggested something

unspeakable. "*Mira, chica,* and who's going to buy the test?" she stage-whispers.

"Uh, we will?" I offer uncertainly.

Mind you, as far as Embarrassing Things to Purchase at the Drugstore goes, a home pregnancy test is pretty high up there on the list, but what can you do? I don't see many other options right now.

Lucy shakes her head again, making as though I am a totally hopeless case. "We can't," she says, sounding sad and resigned. "It's too . . . it's just not done. If anyone were to see us—it's not something that a single girl our age can do. Not here."

"Well, I don't live here," I say, logically enough. "What do I care about my 'rep'? I could just go and buy the thing, couldn't I?"

"You're my cousin. It would reflect on our family," Lucy protests.

I shake my head, frustrated. "This is crazy. You're freaking out, but we can't go get the test because it's awkward?" I ask.

Lucy crosses and uncrosses her arms even more emphatically, further evidence that we're really not operating on the same page. "It's not crazy; it's the way it is here. We can't go buy a test ourselves."

"Fine," I say, resigned. Who am I to tell her what is and

isn't appropriate around here after all? I pause, try to gather my composure. As for alternatives, I can only think of . . . well, one.

And I don't think Lucy will like it one bit.

"No," she tells me.

I don't know how, but she reads my mind.

"We are *not* talking to your mother about this," she tells me.

"Lucy, we have to," I insist. "Someone has to get us a pregnancy test. We can't go to the doctor—fine, I think that's probably not necessary right now anyway. You don't want to buy a test yourself—fine, I guess I don't blame you, although it wouldn't be the *worst* thing in the world. But if those two options are out, then we don't have a whole lot of choices." I pause. "Unless you'd rather tell *your* mother."

Lucy shudders.

"Exactly." I shrug. "My mom's cool—about most stuff," I say, crossing my fingers behind my back and hoping this is as true as I think it is. "And we *know* without a doubt that she will be better about this than Rosa. I mean, really."

"True," Lucy admits, however grudgingly.

"My mom can keep a secret," I say, still with the crossed fingers.

Lucy bites a fingernail. *"Espero que sea la verdad, chica."*

Yeah, I hope so too.

* * *

Mom and Rosa are back by ten, what with them being mom-aged and it being a church event and all. Lucy paces, practically wearing a hole in the living-room carpet, while we wait for Rosa to retreat to her bedroom with her nightly glass of wine, a book, and her reading glasses. My mother sits at the kitchen table with a bottle of water, a pen, and a Tuesday *New York Times* crossword. She likes to do the Mondays and Tuesdays in pen. We hover at the doorway of the kitchen, hemming, hawing, and hedging, until way too much time has passed for us to cling to our "casual" charade.

"What. Is. Going. On?" my mother asks, mildly bemused. She caps her pen, lays it on the table, and turns away from the crossword to regard us. "Since when are you two partners in crime?"

I shoot Lucy a meaningful look, thinking she should be the one to break the situation down for my mother. It's her issue, after all. But no dice. She steps backward, gives me a light shove. Okay, then. It's my show.

My hands feel clammy and I'm breathing at twice the normal rate. *This is for Lucy,* I remind myself. For some reason, that makes it easier to act completely and wildly out of character.

"We have a problem," I say. "We were hoping you could help."

* * *

Twenty minutes later we're in Rosa's car, careening down the main strip toward the twenty-four-hour pharmacy.

I've got to give my mom credit—she was as cool as I hoped she'd be. She listened to the news impassively, turning calmly to Lucy after we'd finished. "The test is for you?"

I can't lie; I'm relieved that she didn't assume it was me. It's not a bad sign, as far as her opinion of me is concerned. Of course, I feel guilty for even thinking that way. What exactly do I think it "says" about Lucy's character?

"We really appreciate this," I gush from the backseat. Lucy sits beside my mother in the front, gnawing frenetically on a fingernail.

"You couldn't go yourself," my mother matter-of-facts.

"That's what I told her," Lucy says, almost managing a half smile. "She didn't believe me."

My mother *tsk-tsks*, waves her hand in my direction dismissively. "Emily, do you have any idea the gossip if someone saw a single girl Lucy's age buying a pregnancy test? Trust me, as it is, if we run into anyone we know, they'll manage to pass along the story. But I'm married, so it's less scandalous."

"It's the same with birth control," Lucy tells me. "Good girls aren't even supposed to know what it is. Using it *is*, like, a double sin."

I am in total disbelief. "So what do you do, then?"

"Don't ask, don't tell," Lucy says. "Rhythm method. Pull and pray. Or get knocked up"—she flinches—"and people find out. It's embarrassing. More than embarrassing. At that point you pretty much better hope the guy marries you."

I'm stunned. Maybe it's naive, and it's not like I didn't realize that things were more . . . *traditional* here, but this feels downright archaic. Girls back home worry about their reputations, sure, but somehow it's not quite the same.

"Well, this is good, then," I say, trying to lighten the mood. "Or were you hoping that Rafael would propose?"

A storm cloud darkens across Lucy's features. "We broke up," she says simply. "Last week."

A lump forms in my throat. Oh.

* * *

My mother buys the test without incident ("At least as far as I know," she tells us, emerging from the Rite Aid thoroughly nonplussed) and drives us straight over to the closest McDonald's. We can't take the test into the house, my mom assures me. Someone might see the box or the stick or Tía Rosa might simply *smell* that something's amiss.

Lucy runs into the bathroom, and we split a super-size fries and a chocolate shake while we wait the requisite three minutes for the test results. I have never felt more like a refugee from an after-school special, the sight of my mother slurping on a fast-food shake lending the whole experience a particularly surreal quality.

Three minutes and fifty-nine seconds later, Lucy ginger-ly digs into her tote bag where the stick is wrapped in thick wads of toilet paper. She tentatively strips away the paper like layers of an onion, and I can tell she is both dying to look and desperate not to look.

The suspense is killing *me*; I can only imagine what it must be doing to Lucy. It takes every ounce of restraint to resist flinging myself across the table and wrenching the stick out of her hands.

Finally the stick is clean and paper free. Lucy bites her lip, wrinkles her forehead, looks up at us. "There's a pink line," she says, her voice hollow.

I squint at the packaging. "One pink line or two?"

"Just the one," Lucy says.

"The test line or the one in the window?"

"Wait—which is supposed to be the test line? I think it's . . . maybe it's . . ."

Mercifully my mother takes the test from Lucy to con-firm. "There's nothing there. In the test window," she con-cludes. "You're not pregnant."

"But I'm usually regular. What if the test is wrong?"

"How late is your period?" my mother asks.

"Two weeks," Lucy says, nervous.

My mother shakes her head. "Nope. This thing would have picked it up. It's designed to pick up trace hormones as early as two days after your missed period."

"Are these things reliable?" I ask, because I know that's what Lucy's thinking.

My mother nods emphatically. "They are. Remember I helped put together the curriculum for Feminism, Law, and Reproductive Biology last semester."

Sometimes I forget that my mother's job is actually really cool.

"So why is it so late?" Lucy asks.

My mother shrugs. "It could be anything, really. Stress, changes in diet . . . all of these things will affect your cycle. And then I'm sure worrying about being pregnant didn't help . . . ironically."

"I guess I have been upset," Lucy admits. "With *abuela* passing and . . . I really never thought that Rafael and I would break up. Ever."

I had assumed that their breakup had something to do with the pregnancy, but the way Lucy's talking now makes me think that there's more to the story, that the pregnancy scare is the end of it rather than the beginning.

"I had a friend who went through the same thing," my mother says. Her voice is far away, and I get the feeling that she's talking more to herself than to either of us, lost in her memory. "At pretty much the same age. And of course, we had no idea what to do. I couldn't very well ask my mother to pick up a test for us."

"So what did you do?" I ask.

"What could I do? Nothing. We didn't have anyone we could go to, and we were young, scared, and naive. We chose the 'duck and cover' technique. You know, we pretended it wasn't happening."

"So you just . . . did *nothing?*" I ask, incredulous, even though of course that's exactly what she just said. My mother, the most responsible person in the world, would never do something like that. Never.

"We did nothing," she says flatly. "After about three months, of course, she started to show. Cecilia—her name was—Cecilia had been very slender, so at a certain point there was no hiding what was going on, no matter how baggy she bought her clothes. Anyway, they shipped her off to have her baby with some distant relatives in the countryside, and then I guess they put the baby up for adoption. Eventually Cecilia came back to school, but she never wanted to talk about it. So we never did."

My mother drums her fingers across the linoleum table-top. I can tell she'd kill for a cigarette. "That was when I knew," she says. "That I had to come to the mainland for college. That I had to go to college. Somewhere . . . there would be more options."

"Is that why . . ." I trail off, not sure I have the guts to ask the question that's been nagging at me. "Is that why you broke ties with Grandma and your family? Why you converted?"

"It's why I met your father, sure," she says. "He was a big hippie back then too, so we kept running into each other at all sorts of rallies and things. It was pretty obvious very early on that we had a lot in common. And then when I got to know him and his values, I really related to them. Being Jewish felt . . . it felt right," she says finally. "In a way that nothing else ever had before."

"So why couldn't you be Jewish and still be connected to your family?" Lucy asks.

For my part, I am simply unable to believe that my mother, who is fiercely loyal to my father, Max, and me, would just turn away from her past like that.

"You're missing the point," she says, a crooked smile on her lips. "I would have loved to be connected to the family. But it wasn't an option. I didn't sever ties with Grandma, sweetie. Grandma severed ties with me."

And suddenly, everything that I thought I had known about my mother is completely and utterly turned around.

Fourteen

Lucy and I decide to go for coffee—that is, to *really* go for coffee this time. Mom tries to protest, telling Lucy to go home and take it easy, but Lucy and I both know that we've got a free pass for the day, and we've both got big, sloppy mountains of pent-up nervous tension to expend.

"Your mom, she's great," Lucy understates, stirring an espresso with telltale intensity.

"She is," I agree, meaning it differently, more fully, than I ever have before.

"I never knew . . . well, I always figured that she was the one who turned away from the family. I assumed that was why my mother said—" She flushes, cuts herself off abruptly.

"Your mother didn't have such nice things to say about

mine." I shrug, trying to let Lucy off the hook. "I guess she didn't approve of my mother's choices."

It was a vicious cycle, I realize. Mom's parents cut her off, her family judges her, and in time she stops reaching out to them. How hard it must have been for my mother to come home now, I realize. Especially knowing that she wasn't going to have a chance to make things right with her own mother.

No wonder she's trying so hard with Rosa. No wonder she's going along with the laundry list of "to-dos."

Maybe—and this is really just a maybe—that's why she was so cool with Lucy. Why she didn't judge. Maybe being back here, helping Lucy out, was her way of reconnecting with her past—but drawing on the person she's become since . . .

Well, since she left.

Maybe.

"Yeah," Lucy replies, snapping me out of my reverie. "And my mom—you know, she's so traditional." She shakes her head, almost in disbelief. "And I think she gives me a hard time."

It occurs to me that Tía Rosa does give Lucy a hard time. The way that Lucy lives, the household chores, the level of responsibility that is expected of her always seemed excessive to me. It never dawned on me that it might seem excessive to Lucy too.

"I owe you an apology," Lucy says.

"For what?" I ask.

"For being such a bitch," she says. I open my mouth to protest, and she laughs and cuts me off. "You know I was. I was, I don't know. . . . From everything my mother told me, I was expecting you to be this spoiled brat from New York."

"Which I sort of was," I say, cringing to think of how resentful I was when we first arrived.

"Yeah, but I didn't make it any easier. It was a weird situation. I could have handled it better."

"We both could have," I say, knowing that it's the truth.

The moment is starting to feel a little too Dr. Phil for my taste, but there's something more that I need to ask. "Why did you break up with Rafael?"

It's none of my business, and I can't believe how uncharacteristically nosy I'm being, but what the hell. I'm really curious, and there's no guarantee that Lucy will ever be this open with me again. So it's sort of now or never.

"Oh, you know, the usual stuff," she says. "We had been together for so long, it was starting to feel like we were one person."

I frown. Isn't that the whole point of being with someone? Getting close to them? "I thought that was a good thing."

"Yeah. I mean, I guess it's what you want eventually. But this isn't eventually. I'm barely out of high school. I need to figure myself out before I'm attached at the hip . . . to *anyone*."

It occurs to me that perhaps I haven't given Lucy enough credit.

"He was so pissed," she continues, more to herself than to me. "And the girls . . . well, everyone thinks I'm making a huge mistake. In Puerto Rico you have your boyfriend and you stay with him and eventually you marry him and you have babies." She flinches on the word *babies*.

"Yeah," I say, as though I get it, even though I so don't. But I'm trying to. I'm definitely trying to.

"You've got a boyfriend back home?"

I nod. "Yeah. Or, well, a something." I frown. "It's ending, I think. We're both going off to different colleges and . . . we've been avoiding talking about it. But yeah. It's ending." As I say the words out loud, I know that they're true. "Ugh. I have to call him. I hate having things up in the air." Which of course is how they've been all summer. Shana Rivers can have him, I tell myself. Then I realize I'm slightly bitter, slightly sad, and nostalgic. But definitely ready to make a decisive move.

"You're a little bit into Ricky," Lucy says. It's not a question.

"It's confusing," I tell her.

"I know. But he's my friend. And he's a good guy. So just . . . don't hurt him," she says.

She turns back to her espresso, and I can see that the subject is closed.

* * *

Later that night I steal outside to the pool to call Noah. He answers quickly, on the second ring, so quickly that I guess he's been napping on the sofa in front of some game or another. The blaring television in the background tells me that I guess right. "Hey," I say, willing my resolve not to crumble.

"What's going on, babe?" he asks blearily.

"Oh, it was a crazy day," I say. "Lucy was, um, sick." It's easier than getting into a long story, and besides, it's Lucy's story anyway.

"So did you have to, like, do all of her chores for her and stuff?" he asks, like he thinks that's maybe a little bit funny.

"Well, I helped out, sure," I say. "But not, you know, more than usual."

"Mmm-hmm," he mumbles. It's obvious he's concentrating on the game. Good. That makes this easier.

"Look, I was thinking I'd love to get together when I come home," I say. "We haven't seen each other in so long."

"Sure, of course," he says.

"But I mean, we both know that I won't be coming

home for another few weeks. So . . . I don't know. . . . And with how we're both going away to college in September . . ." I swallow, hoping he'll pick up on what I'm not saying.

"Yeah," he says shortly. "I was thinking that too."

He was? "You were?"

"Yeah. But, uh, I wasn't sure, so I didn't want to say anything."

"Right, well. I mean, I wish it were different; I wish I were home"—as I say the words, I realize that they're actually not true at all—"but I'm not. So maybe we should just plan on seeing each other . . . when we see each other," I finish lamely.

He clears his throat. "Is there—I mean, is there someone down there?"

"Like am I seeing someone?" I ask.

I think of Ricky and the almost kiss. It was Ricky who tried to kiss me rather than the other way around, but it's not as though I hadn't given the idea any thought.

"No," I tell him. Then a horrible thought strikes me. "Are you?"

"No," he assures me.

But maybe he's not seeing, oh, say, Shana Rivers the same way I didn't kiss Ricky. But sort of wanted to. I push the image out of my mind. At this point it hardly matters.

"Right, cool," I say. "Well, uh, I have to get back inside"—not true—"but I'll call you. . ."

I realize that we've just broken up, and suddenly I have no idea how to finish that sentence.

"Yeah," Noah says. "Um, good-bye."

"Bye," I say. I hang up the phone and stare at it, blue LCD screen glowing in my palm. For a moment I'm swept with the urge to call him again, to take it all back, to tell him we should be together forever.

But the moment passes, and I go back inside.

* * *

I call Ade and Izzy to tell them what happened—with Noah, I mean, not with Lucy. They're both sympathetic, but Isabelle definitely seems a little more distant than Ade. It's typical, but I find that it bothers me less than it typically does. Interesting.

Lucy finds me in the living room, sitting on the couch and staring off into space at nothing. "It's done," she guesses.

I nod glumly, sigh. "Stick a fork in it." I look up at her. "I feel weird about it," which is about as close to accurate as I can get.

"Tell me about it," she says. "I told Rafael about the test and he was relieved, but he wants to see me."

"You don't want to see him?"

"I'm not ready yet. We're going to have to see each other sooner or later—I mean, all of our friends hang out together; that's one of the sucky things about breaking up with someone you've been with, like, forever." She pauses. "But, you know. Not today."

"I get it," I say, because I really, really do.

Lucy grins at me suddenly, her eyes lighting up in a way that I didn't expect. "You know what we need?"

"Chocolate," I tell her. "Chocolate, cheese, and ice cream." My standard depression diet.

"Salsa," she clarifies.

"You mean, like with chips?" I ask, confused.

"No, silly." She laughs. "Dancing."

"Oh, no," I say, shaking my head emphatically. "No, no, no."

She leans over, grabs my arms, tugs me until I'm finally standing upright. "Oh, yes. Yes, yes, yes."

Fifteen

We sneak out, of course. Lucy's got it down to an art form; I feel like Jennifer Garner or some other action heroine. She knows exactly where to step to avoid creaks in the floor, exactly how wide to push open the door, exactly the right angle at which to shimmy through the doorway. And when it comes to backing her car out of the driveway, she's like a criminal mastermind. I'm somewhat awed.

The club is packed tonight, and for once I've got the dress code down. I still wouldn't be caught dead in white pants—I don't care how trendy they are; they are not my finest look butt-wise—but I've got a bright, tangerine-colored halter on that looks like Lucy lite. Of course, being well costumed doesn't make me feel any less self-conscious when Lucy drags me out to the center of the dance floor. Pia, Ramona, and Teresa are there, hooting and whooping in the background.

I stumble around at first—it's been years since tap and ballet lessons, and I don't really know how helpful those would be now anyway. Lucy laughs and shakes her head in mock despair. She pulls a Patrick Swayze and instructs me to follow her feet. I promptly step forward and clock her with my huge, Cro-Magnon forehead. Has my cranium always been so massively misshapen? I'm like the Elephant Man, if he were also rhythmically challenged.

Lucy only laughs harder, and suddenly I realize that I'm laughing too. She twirls me in, out, does a little cha cha cha that's half camp, half elegance, and total Lucy. To my sheer and utter amazement, I find myself imitating her, though I know I still need practice. Ramona catcalls from the side-lines.

Pia, Ramona, and Teresa step forward, flanking Lucy on either side as she moves backward. They form a small circle and begin weaving in, out, and around each other. Before I can feel left out, though, I'm whirled in the opposite direction, spun, and dipped. I look up.

It's Ricky.

I stagger slightly, and we go down. He's left lying on top of me in a heap, and it's so awkward, so absurd, so totally ridiculous that we both lose it completely, laughing hysterically until I'm wiping tears from the corners of my eyes. I can't remember ever laughing this hard. It feels good.

No, it feels *great*.

"Come outside," he shouts, leaning in to be heard over the music. "I need some fresh air."

Ricky's idea of "fresh air" is lighting a cigarette and sucking it down greedily, like it's a glass of water and he's just pitched a tent on the sun. "Nice," I say, gesturing at the cigarette disapprovingly.

"I'm quitting," he says, grinning. "Besides, how many times have you seen me smoke since you got here?"

"Good point," I say. "Okay, just this once."

He puffs away and we stand side by side in comfortable silence. "I can't even remember the last time I had one," Ricky comments. He squints as if trying to spot a faraway point on the horizon. He must remember then, because his face falls. "I guess I've just been tense . . . lately. . . ."

"Oh," I say. "Right." He's not saying it point-blank, but I understand what he's getting at. We both pause. "Look, about that night—" I begin, when I absolutely can't stand the tension.

"It's okay," he says, waving his free hand at me. "You have a boyfriend." He flushes. "I mean, not that it's, um, the only reason you wouldn't—"

"Don't worry." I toss him a lifeline.

"Right, but I mean, the point is that I knew about your boyfriend. So it was pretty sketchy to try anything. I guess I just got caught up. I hope you don't think I'm sleazy or anything."

"Of course not," I assure him. "Maybe I was sending mixed signals. Noah and I were in sort of a holding pattern."

"Were?" he asks.

"Yeah, we broke up. That's why Lucy brought me out tonight. We both needed some cheering up."

"Good thing Rafael decided to stay home, huh?" Ricky asks.

"Right," I say. I stare at Ricky and all at once adore him even more than I would have thought possible. He doesn't react at all to the news of my newfound singledom, doesn't say anything that would make me feel pressured or uncomfortable. The question of kissing him comes back to me like a hazy watercolor, not something I am quite ready for just here and now, but a free-form possibility. If and when the time is right.

I realize that I trust myself to know when the time is right.

"Well," Ricky says, finishing his cigarette and stomping it out underneath his sneaker, "shall we?"

"We shall," I say agreeably.

He holds his arm out for me like Fred Astaire or some other icon of a classier age. I link my arm through his, and we return to the club.

* * *

The light is on in the living room when we return home. I shoot Lucy a look as she kills the engine, coasts into the driveway.

She shrugs. "What are we gonna do?" she asks. I can't think of a way to get from the back door to our bedrooms without passing the living room. We're busted.

Oh, well. Even if Tía Rosa grounds us—and I'm pretty sure that she will—it was totally worth it. We get out of the car and lock it up, head off to meet our doom.

But it's my mother, not Tía Rosa, in the living room, still with a pen-level crossword. She looks up at us as we sheepishly tiptoe past. I brace for a rebuke, but it doesn't come. Instead my mother does something curious indeed: she winks. "Can't sleep."

I wrinkle my forehead in confusion, but I'm not about to look a gift horse in the mouth. "Yeah, neither could we."

She grins. "You'd better get to bed before Rosa wakes up." And that's it; she's back to her crossword.

So we do.

* * *

Two weeks later Rosa has a huge dinner for our entire

extended Puerto Rican family. It's like the wake all over again, except minus my father and Max, and this time it's a happy occasion. The house teems with brown-skinned faces, long, lacquered fingernails, backwards baseball caps, beer, sangria, rum, and for the minors, punch.

"*Ay, mami*, you made the sangría?" José calls to me.

"*Sí*, señor," I reply. "Lucy and I were soaking and chopping fruit all morning." It's true; I have the stained fingertips to prove it.

"Not bad, *muchacha*. Not bad for a gringa," he says, teasing.

"Excuse me," I say huffily. "I believe you mean *nuyorican.*"

José's girlfriend, finally here in what must be the single most marathon incident of meet-the-family, giggles beside him and snuggles up against him. Her name is Angela, and she looks a little bit like Jessica Alba. She's so soft-spoken and friendly that it's impossible not to like her. It's also impossible not to see just how much José adores her. And I give her huge credit for being here, for not being overwhelmed by all of us.

I give me huge credit for not being overwhelmed by all of us. Or, really, for just being us.

"Emily, *que tal*?" It's Juan, Eva's youngest.

"*Nada mucho,*" I say. "*¿Y tú?*"

"Eh, work is crazy," he says, matter-of-fact. He's a mechanic, Lucy told me. It sounds like the sort of thing that isn't much fun when it's crazy. But he seems not to mind too much. "So, you're going home tomorrow. Time flies, huh? Tell me, *nuyorican*, are you sorry to be going back?"

Lucy passes by toting a platter of *plátanos*. I eagerly spear one. "She's not going," she says, overhearing the tail end of our conversation. "Change of plans."

"Lucy got me a job working at the mall with her," I say. "So I'm going to stay here for the rest of the summer. I'm going to share Lucy's room."

With Isabelle and Adrienne gone, there wasn't much for me to do back home but get a job, so no reason, my mother and I decided, that I couldn't just work down in Puerto Rico.

Tía Rosa was fine with it since, as she put it, I've been such a *milagro*, a miracle around the house.

That's me, miraculous.

"*Espérate*, you have to hear the best part," Lucy says, dashing quickly outdoors to deposit the platter down on the buffet. She runs back in, slightly out of breath. "We're going on a road trip before school starts. The end of August. We're gonna do the chick bonding thing. Like *Thelma and Louise*. With no suicide at the end."

"But maybe *with* Brad Pitt," I chime. "Or a reasonable facsimile."

"Bring on the hotties!" Lucy says, doing an excited little dance in place.

"Rosa's letting you do that?" Juan asks, incredulous. "No way."

Lucy nods. "I know, I couldn't believe it either. But *Gloria* spoke to her."

From where we stand, I can see my mother through the kitchen window, holding a glass of punch and gesturing animatedly, responding to something that Rosa is saying.

"So, Emily doesn't get to go cross-country this summer, but she does get to see the Puerto Rican countryside," Lucy says, amiable. "It's the next-best thing."

She's wrong, of course. About it being the next-best thing. It's not. It's just different. Way, way different than I had imagined my summer ending. But it's certainly not a consolation prize. I smile at Lucy. "You have no idea," I say. "Nada."

About the Author

Micol Ostow is half Puerto Rican, half Jewish, half editor, half writer, half chocolate, half peanut butter. When she's under deadline she's often half asleep. She believes that the sum is greater than the parts except in the case of Chubby Hubby ice cream. She lives in New York City where she reads, runs, and drinks way too much coffee. Visit Micol at micolostow.com.

Acknowledgments

Muchas gracias to Eloise Flood, Kristen Pettit, and all of the Razorbills for being amazing friends and inspiring colleagues alike; to Bonnie Bader, Jon Goodspeed, and Debra Dorfman for supporting my moonlighting and never complaining when I get to work late; to Kristen Kemp for a much-needed kick in the tail; to my dad, who taught me everything I needed to know about Jewish guilt and new-wave Zionism (separate but related!); to my brother David, a genuine *nuyorican* and the most interesting person I know; to my grandfather Morty and in memory of my grandmother Miriam, who have taught me never to settle for anything less than excellence; to the greater Ostow clan and all of my friends (who are far too indulgent, I must say); to Jodi Reamer, for endless good faith; and to Noah, for unprecedented levels of awesomeosity and big-time laughs.